The
Ruby

Kate Brown Fisher

PublishAmerica
Baltimore

ISBN: 1-59286-293-4
PUBLISHED BY
PUBLISHAMERICA BOOK PUBLISHERS
www.publishamerica.com
Baltimore

Printed in the United States of America

Nothing that is good in my life could ever have been possible without God! Whenever a door closed and I thought that was the end, God opened another door, and sometimes two. Some others that deserve credit are:

Of course my mother, father, brothers, husband, children, writing group friends, and many more that are too numerous to mention. I sincerely thank you!

To Maura
God Bless!
Kate Fisher

Acknowledgements

Titanic, An Illustrated History by Don Lynch
Molly Brown, Unraveling the Myth by Kristen Iverson
A Night to Remember by Walter Lord

Chapter 1

Mary Kate McKinney was amazed as her blue eyes were fixed on the largest object she had ever seen. She was told it was the grandest ship in all history, and she couldn't believe she was really going to America on this inspiring means of transport to start her new life.

Mary Kate pulled a picture out of her gray flannel coat pocket. William Richter's face stared back at her from the dog-eared photograph he mailed her. This was the first time Mary Kate had ever traveled out of Ireland, and no one knew when she would be back. Thank God Patrick, her brother, was with her. Shoving the picture back in her pocket, Mary Kate tried to dispel her uncertainty.

"You scared?" Patrick stared up at the massive iron ship that protruded into the overcast sky.

"No, excited, but not afraid." Mary Kate turned to her brother, her blue eyes sparking with emotion.

"Yes, you are!" Patrick laughed in his abrasive voice as he patted his sister on the gray cap that crowned her glorious auburn curls and took her gloved hand in his.

The pair walked up the quickly crowding dock on a beautiful April morning. The hazy sunshine broke through intermittently on this marvel of modern wonders called *Titanic*. The brother and sister took turns pointing out the sizes and shapes of everything on her.

Titanic was the pride of the White Star Line. Her stately colors were magnificent, stark white, red, and black. Her wide buff yellow funnels would soon be spewing black smoke that came forth from the massive coalbunkers in the bottom part of the ship that any one rarely sees. When she set sail at noon, she would make her historic maiden voyage.

At half past nine, the dock at Southampton was a maddening sea of people. Some people were there to be passengers on this grand steamer; but many others were there just out of curiosity or to wish a loved one good-bye. Merchants of all types and bustling crewmembers busied themselves at the foot of this great ship.

A twinge of remorse pinched Mary Kate as she witnessed one girl giving her father a good-bye kiss. Part of her just wanted to turn around and go home and she felt as if she were watching herself and her own father the day she and Patrick left Ireland.

Patrick huffed on his stubby cigarette, the other hand holding a worn leather suitcase that carried all of his and his sister's possessions they could take to America as Mary Kate clutched her book in one hand. Two of their uncles were priests, and they had taught all McKinney children to read, starting with the bible. Unable to understand her fascination with books, Patrick was proud that his sister was so smart, and he knew she would make a good husband for that American man.

"Now, when it comes time to board, you stay with me," Patrick warned her, shaking his cigarette at her and then putting it out on the dusty dock. Mary Kate simply nodded and smiled. She was proud of her oldest brother. He looked handsome in his new suspenders and new brown cap that matched his eyes, like a real grown man. The money their family had was sparse, especially since their mother had died when Mary Kate was very little.

That left their father to work hard and raise the five children by himself at the same time. But Keeran McKinney had been kind enough to supply a few new things for Mary Kate and Patrick to begin their life anew in America. Since neither of them would be back to Ireland until who knew when, their father also convinced them it was better to board at the ship's actual disembarkation in Southern England. Knowing that she would miss her father and her other three brothers, Mary Kate hoped that someday she could afford to bring them over to visit. It helped to know that they were all happy for her and hopeful for Patrick. The thought didn't make her any less tense, but she knew this travel experience would change her life forever.

Mostly American first-class ladies began to come by, bedecked with bright shiny jewels and big feathery hats. Almost all of them had a furry stole or coat. Shining brass-clad trunks stuffed to the brim with more glamorous garb, carried by stewards, ensued the ladies up to the ship. Mary Kate stared after them with awe, as people like that were rare in Ireland, and their haughty presence astounded her.

Anxiety mounted as time came closer to board this fantastic new vessel. Patrick buttoned up his wool brown coat and lit another cigarette, the smoke curling about his reddish-brown head.

Patrick knelt down by the edge of the dock, fingering the rope that was so thick he could barely get his hand around it. "Look at the size of these ropes!"

"Well, they say she is the biggest ship ever," Mary Kate chimed in.

"Now, I know it's true." Patrick raised one red eyebrow at his sister, who laughed at her mischievous brother. They headed down to the third-class gangway, where passengers were beginning to board the ship.

Matthew Burnes checked his gold pocketwatch. Nearly half past nine on Wednesday morning, and boredom was settling in.

He shut his book and set it on the tattered train seat beside him. The train click-clacked rhythmically as it made its way towards Southampton to travel back across the ocean towards home. Matthew writhed with anticipation about going back to America. Oxford had been a diversion created by his parents, who now were sending him home to run his father's chain of coalmines. Matthew's father, Charles Burnes, had made his fortune in mining and wanted his children to take over his large and very profitable business. Pigeonholed into being his father's protégé, Matthew was the youngest child and the only son in a family of four other siblings.

Matthew feared running the mines, because he wasn't as hard-nosed as his father. Where Charles Burnes was business-minded, Matthew was people-minded. Matthew had seen the horrid conditions his father's workers endured, and he wasn't sure he could consciously let people face those dangers just to earn a meager existence.

The recent coal strike had set Matthew's father into response, and he had sent for his son as soon as possible. His father had written him a letter, telling him there was no reason to stay in Europe any longer. Matthew yawned, rubbed his eyes, and looked resentfully across the seat at his family's butler, Thomas, who had come from Pennsylvania to bring Matthew home. Of all his parents' servants, it was Thomas that Matthew disliked the most. He was drunk, rude, and bitter towards the world, obviously refusing to see his shortcomings. Matthew was sure his parents probably sent Thomas so they could be rid of the slobbish man for two weeks. Bored, Matthew reached in his deep coat pockets and pulled out two first-class tickets for that new ship, *Titanic*.

Matthew sighed and scratched his clean-shaven square chin as he studied the tickets, when a young woman walked by whom he recognized instantly.

"Virginia!" he cried, jumping out of his seat. The dark-haired young woman spun around, and a warm smile came over her face.

"Why, Matthew!" His younger cousin ran towards him and hugged him tightly.

"I can't believe it! Are you here to board *Titanic* too?" he asked, pleasantly surprised.

"Yes, I'm going to see David off," Virginia said, her green eyes brimming with mischief. Matthew looked at her with a curious face.

"Oh, I'm sorry, I forgot you had been away. David is a young American man I met here in England at Grampa's dock. He's going back to America to be a salesman for Grampa's machines. That's him, isn't he great?" Virginia grabbed her cousin's arm and pointed eagerly down the aisle to a tall and handsome young man who was facedown in the paper.

Matthew asked, confused. "So are you traveling or just seeing off?"

"Well, I brought some things with me, but let's just say I didn't tell Grampa I was going back to America so soon!" Matthew laughed and shook his head at his cousin, who had always managed to cause a stir, whether it was with her beauty or her free spirit.

The cousins parted ways and promised to see each other on board. Matthew looked over at Thomas, who had been watching the cousins with interest, and the indolent butler rustled his newspaper and continued reading. Matthew's stomach sank when he thought about spending the next week with this man. He sat back down on the seat, praying it would go fast.

Matthew finally stepped off the train onto the dock after the endless ride. The air seemed a bit crisp that morning, and the sea breeze tingled his nose. He donned his brown bowler cap and squinted his green eyes to the hazy English sunshine. He waited for Thomas, who was always dallying behind.

"He's as fat as a frog and always lagging about," Matthew muttered under his breath. Thomas came lumbering clumsily down the narrow doorway to exit the train. Sighing impatiently, Matthew continued silently down the dock, that was crowded to the hilt with people.

Stewards were there to quickly take care of the baggage, and Matthew draped his coat over one arm and clasped his book in the same hand.

Rounding the corner from where the train had let off its passengers, Matthew wasn't quite prepared for the sight that came into view. His eyes enveloped a long wall of black; the body of this glorious new vessel blocked his view of the ocean from the dock.

The ships funnels hissed steam as its coal bunkers were being stoked in preparation for her great journey that would soon begin.

Matthew stared in awe at this astonishing sight. He had heard stories of her grandeur but was skeptical until he now set eyes on her himself. He motioned for Thomas to follow as he bumped through the energetic crowd towards the first class gangway.

"Tickets, please!" the young crewman cried out as the two men entered the new ship.

Fishing through his coat pockets for the tickets, Matthew handed them to the young man.

"All right, here is your map of the ship, sir. Go down the corridor...." The crewman explained in detail the route to the stateroom on 'B' deck.

Matthew thanked him, and he and Thomas followed the precise directions to the room.

Once inside the lavish room, Matthew draped his brown coat over the plush chair. He had no time to pay attention to the ornate details of the room but ran to the modern bathroom, complete with a flushable stool, sink, and bathtub. He could scarcely believe how modern it all was for a ship; it was a floating hotel. Matthew had no more tested the toilet when, seconds later, a knock came at the door and the baggage arrived.

"You can put most of it in the hold, but I will take those three there." Matthew pointed at the three suitcases that the steward quickly brought inside the room. Tipping the steward generously, Matthew closed the door quietly.

The stateroom was two small bedrooms connected by a common parlor area. Pleased by the separate bedrooms, Matthew chuckled to himself when he thought how unbearable it would have to be *that* close to Thomas the whole trip.

Matthew resentfully unpacked his things as he looked out the large, clear window at the sea that moved far beyond his view.

America is over there, and then my life becomes meaningless, Matthew thought unhappily. Thomas had settled in on the settee in the parlor area and was dozing peacefully without a care in the world. Matthew wondered how much his lazy butler had already had tipped from his bottle this morning.

Finally finished unpacking his things, Matthew decided to lie down on the bed and read, and within seconds, he was asleep on the starchy fresh white bedsheets. He slept through the whole ordeal of the launching, until late that evening.

The line seemed to be endless, and it crept along slowly up the long gangway as people and bags lumbered along wanting to board the massive steamer. Mary Kate craned her neck to see in front of her and notice crewmembers handing out maps of the ship.

The brother and sister finally entered the ship of destiny and experienced a new feeling of awe. Everything on board gleamed white, and the woodwork glowed majestically as if to mirror the hopes of her passengers. Electric lights blazed from every panel, something Mary Kate and Patrick had never seen.

Fiddling with the map, Patrick soon deciphered that they needed to go to the stern of the ship on 'F' deck. Mary Kate followed Patrick closely against the flow of traffic down to their cabin. Their berth was small and had only one set of bunks, a small commode, and an even smaller space for their suitcase. Single men and women were not normally put together, but since they were brother and sister, it was allowed.

Patrick smoothed his thick red moustache in the mirror as Mary Kate tossed her book on the bottom bunk. Patrick looked over at his sister and smiled, knowing she was very excited and nervous about this trip to America.

"Don't you want to go on deck and see her pull away?" Patrick put his hand on her arm as she started to unbutton her long gray coat.

"I guess so." Mary Kate nodded.

"C'mon, Sis, this is once in a lifetime!" Patrick teased her. Smiling, she and Patrick took off for the boat deck, hands clasped, winding their way back through the crowded hallways and stairways.

Everything looked small from the deck of the giant ship. Leaning over the rail and looking at the sea of faces below, Mary Kate noticed that some were sad, others happy.

Patrick lit a cigarette and stood up on the rail next to his sister. His brown eyes lit up as the funnels began to spew black smoke. The din of voices was almost deafening to their ears as the excitement pierced the air. The cold air stung Mary Kate's white face, but she didn't care. Almost everyone around her beamed with happiness and excitement. The air was chilly, but her heart was warm inside. The massive engines roared to life underneath their feet, and soon the foghorn blared to announce *Titanic*'s departure away into history. The modern world was floating away into a new one filled with the wonder of technology. Mary Kate suddenly couldn't believe she was here!

Her feet were standing on the largest ship ever built! She was a part of history, herself. Overcome with joy and excitement, she let out a small giggle and began to wave frantically, joining the rest of the passengers on deck. Patrick looked at his sister and laughed. She really was going to America, and it all started now! Shouts and choruses of happy voices filled the air like a thousand drums as everyone watched the ship sail bravely down the Southampton waterway into a new world.

Titanic glided down the channel uninterrupted until she passed two ships moored together and not in service because of the coal strike. Both *New York* and *Oceanic*'s decks were filled with onlookers trying to catch an eyeful of the world's largest unsinkable ship. The ship nearest *Titanic*'s port side, *New York*, began to swing out in front of her. *New York*'s massive ropes pulled tight, then snapped back, causing the mass of people to run from their recoil. A rush caused by *Titanic*'s port propeller kept the stray ship from hitting her by only feet. Running out along the bow of their tugboat, two seamen threw a rope to the stray ship, which was thankfully retreating and making way for the larger vessel.

The men in the tugboat looked warily at each other. *Titanic* was too big to move swiftly around objects in its path.

The near-collision was missed, and soon the passengers on *Titanic* soon resumed their normal travelling activities.

Later that afternoon, Mary Kate sat in the nearly empty third-class general area, reading her book. A young man sat down at the table across from her, and he took a slurp of whatever he was drinking. Mary Kate looked up at him and met his dark eyes. She smiled shyly as he removed his hat.

Not uncomely, Mary Kate sensed the man knew that about himself. She wondered why he had to sit next to her in the practically uninhabited room.

"How are you today, young miss?" the young man asked cheerfully, setting his cup back on its saucer with a clank. His British accent gave away his origins.

"Oh, very fine, thank you," Mary Kate answered politely in her own Irish drawl, her blue eyes darting up from her book.

"Well, if I were you, I would get off this ship at the next stop," he whispered over to her quietly.

Mary Kate looked at the young man inquisitively. "May I ask why?"

Setting down his tea, the stranger removed his black leather gloves and set them next to his hat on the table. "This ship is cursed." He picked up his tea and resumed his dainty slurping.

Mary Kate never traveled before today, and was not use to strangers' quirks. She wasn't sure what this man was about to say, or why he was even going to say it.

"I see you like to read," the strange man continued, "have you ever heard of a book called *Futility*?"

"Pardon me?" Mary Kate thought he was changing the subject.

"Well, it's a book about a ship. A ship called *Titan*. Supposedly the biggest and grandest ship in the whole world that is supposed to be unsinkable. But in this book, the ship hits an iceberg in the North Atlantic and sinks. That little incident back there where we almost hit that other ship was enough to make me realize that the little book may have some truth. I am getting off in Queenstown, and heading back to London immediately." The strange young man smacked his lips as he finished his tea.

Mary Kate knew she should pass the man off as a paranoid stranger, but the parallels between the two ships were making sense. But what if he made it up? She excused herself quickly and headed back to her cabin. Dismissing the British man and his words as those of a fearsome traveler, she wouldn't give it any more thought.

Light outside the porthole faded to dusky amber as *Titanic* headed into Cherbourg, France, about an hour later than scheduled. Much too large to dock at this site, some of the richest passengers who would board *Titanic* were being ferried to her from shore by a ship named *Nomadic*.

Patrick swore he heard the huge anchor drop on her, staring out the porthole. He turned to Mary Kate and smiled, rubbing his thick moustache thoughtfully.

"Ya hungry yet?" he asked her. Mary Kate nodded and set her book down on the small bottom bunk. The siblings stood up and went to supper in the third-class general area. Fancier and far more than either Patrick or Mary Kate had at home, the servings on this ship were so large that Mary Kate couldn't finish her plate and shared what was left with her brother, who was ravenous for the hot, delicious meal.

After supper, Patrick suggested they go up to the boat deck and see the ocean at night.

Mary Kate's eyes widened in fear. "Oh, Patrick, but it's so dark though...."

Patrick just laughed at his sister's hesitance and grabbed her hand. He pulled them onto the boat deck of the large ship, which was finally steaming away again. Both were awed by the blackness around them. If it weren't for the lights coming from the first-class verandah café, they would have been in total darkness.

"C'mon down here!" Patrick called. They headed for the stern of the ship, and as they headed away from the lights, they could see many stars twinkling above them like new fallen snowflakes.

"Wow." Mary Kate could say no more. She held on to the rail and stood up, her feet on the bottom rail. She leaned her head back and let the ocean breeze whip past her face. Her stomach was tickled as the ocean moved rhythmically underneath her, and she let the moment melt in her memory.

She could faintly hear a piano and violin from the palm court, the occasional flirtatious laughter of a lady through the open windows, and the clicking of heels on the wooden boat deck. The massive wake caused by the ship's large propellers rushed through her ears. The air smelled salty, but not the same as the ocean near Ireland. It smelled exciting and fresh tonight, something else new to experience in this day of firsts for her.

Stepping off the rail, the cold fresh air stung Mary Kate's face. She looked over at her brother, who had found a spot on a wrought iron and wooden bench. He was snoring loudly, his cigarette still smoking in his hand. Mary Kate laughed and shook her head. It was his idea to come up here, and she was the one enjoying it! She quietly walked over to her brother and pounced on him.

"Oh Damn!" Patrick hollered, and he sprang up. He saw Mary Kate standing over him, holding her stomach and laughing. Patrick shook his head and stepped out his cigarette. "C'mon, let's get to bed." Patrick took his sister's shoulders and led her back to their cabin in the belly of the ship.

Matthew's cousin, Virginia, smiled flirtatiously at her fiancé, David. Not being under the watchful eye of their grandfather, she felt free to peruse the limits of her mischievous feelings.

David was oblivious to her advances as he and Matthew discussed some of the ship's finer appointments with White Star Line's finest captain, E.J. Smith. This was Captain Smith's final journey before his retirement. They all felt lucky to be included with the captain, who was a good friend of Matthew and Virginia's grandfather.

Captain Smith felt comfortable with his young crew, and that the pinnacle of his career would be one filled with delight and relaxation.

Yawning, Matthew sat back in the large dining chair. To him, this was nothing more than rich people strutting like proud peacocks. The older he got, the less he could tolerate it.

"Excuse me." Matthew pushed his chair backward with a squeak and stood up abruptly. Everyone at the table stared at the good-looking young man inquisitively.

"See you later in the smoking room?" David asked politely in his pleasant voice, he had already become fond of his fiancée's cousin, though he'd only known him a few short hours.

"I believe I'm going to bed, but thank you." Matthew gave a short bow to David and gave his cousin a short smile before leaving the well-lit first-class dining saloon.

Flopping on the bed, Matthew undid his vest and tie. *All dressed up for nothing,* he thought as he dropped his gold cufflinks on the dresser. He had traveled the Atlantic a few times, going back and forth to school. He had seen the dark ocean at night and daybreak on the water. He would have to be ready for the responsibility of running the mines when he got back to America, and he was sure that his mother would have ten girls lined up; girls that were ripe and primed for marriage. What better way to settle down than with a woman? Matthew didn't want to settle for anyone, though. He wanted to find someone who could challenge him intellectually and someone he could have some fun with. Those descriptions certainly didn't fit any of the girls he grew up with. Where would he ever find someone he could truly love?

Matthew sighed and looked out his porthole at nothing: just calm, dark ocean. He leaned over and pulled his book out of the top dresser drawer. He could hear Thomas snoring in the next bedroom over.

The snoring was too loud, and soon Matthew couldn't concentrate on the words in his book. Exasperated, he slammed his book shut with a thump and turned out the lamp. His dreams were filled with nightmares of miners under his command, trapped down deep in the earth.

Chapter 2

The next morning, the ship stopped briefly about noon in Queenstown, Ireland. More than once Mary Kate thought that she could just sneak off the ship and go back home to her dad and her brothers. That wouldn't be fair to Patrick, though, or to William, who she had promised to marry.

More passengers climbed on board even though *Titanic* still wasn't at her full capacity, and she was finally on her way across the Atlantic Ocean, nothing but blue water for miles. She was steaming at a very good clip, and the ride was smooth. People who had previously felt seasick felt very comfortable on this ship.

Third-class passengers could use most of the facilities, but usually kept to "their" parts of the ship. One of which consisted of the poop deck on the very stern of the ship. There were nicely slatted park benches lining the deck, so one could sit and just enjoy the ocean breezes. The third-class general area was another popular place where many passengers stayed to write letters to relatives on the White Star Line stationery, boasting how they were sailing to America on this newest of all modern liners. A young crewmember had been nice enough to let Mary Kate and Patrick peek in the gymnasium from the boat deck. People's amazement at the technology of this floating palace never waned.

Thursday, Mary Kate and Patrick busied themselves touring the ship and standing on deck, feeling the sea breeze. Sad that his sister would have very few carefree moments when she got to America, their father had told Patrick how very stuffy William Richter actually was in some of his letters. Only letting Mary Kate read and respond to a few of the letters, Keeran McKinney was resolute that this may be the one chance for anyone in their family to better themselves. Patrick still worried his sister would spend the rest of her life under her new husband's thumb.

Friday morning, Patrick was up early and ready to go up on the poop deck for a little fresh air and sunshine, and the morning's first cigarette. As he stood in the hallway outside his cabin, he made a short grunt as he noticed he was out of smokes.

"Patrick! Is that you?" a familiar Irish voice asked behind him. Patrick turned around to the unmistakable voice of his friend Sean.

"Sean, man! What are you doin' here?" Patrick clapped his friend on the back as he approached him. Sean laughed and walked alongside Patrick in the narrow hallway.

Sean and his brother Ryan were childhood friends from the same small town as Mary Kate and Patrick. They had boarded in Queenstown the day before.

"Our father is sending us to America, he can't afford us anymore. So, what brings you here?" Sean wiped away the strawberry blond wisps from his eyes. Patrick shrugged and explained the ordeal of his Aunt Opal arranging Mary Kate's marriage to a young Boston man. Sean listened with interest as the boys came out on deck.

"I'm not really sure if this is for the best or not," Patrick said sadly.

"Oh?"

"I just wonder what Mary Kate's life will be like after all this happens. It was all Opal's idea, and I think Mary Kate feels she must do this because it's family."

"I know she would do anything you and your brothers tell

22

her is the right thing to do." Sean smiled sympathetically at his friend.

"Yes, I know. That's why it worries me so." Patrick's brown eyes looked down at the decking. He had forgotten he was out of smokes.

"Ahhh, Jesus. I forgot. Where does a guy buy smokes around here?" Sean laughed at his friend as they continued their walk.

Mary Kate and Patrick decided to rest in their cabin after lunch. Picking up her book, she lay down on the top bunk to read. Patrick yawned and stared blankly out the porthole. A sharp tap came at the door, and the siblings exchanged confused glances.

"Open up! It's Sean and Ryan!" came the muffled voice from outside the door. Patrick rushed over to the door and let his friends inside.

"Hey, guys, come in! Come in!" Patrick opened the door and let his two friends inside.

Mary Kate looked up from her book on the bottom bunk and greeted them. She quickly went back to her book.

"What are ya readin' there, Katie?" Sean, the younger brother, asked. Mary Kate looked up and sighed.

"It's *Oliver Twist*, by Dickens. Ya interested in books really, Sean?"

"Just didn't want to leave you out, that's all," Sean replied honestly, then turned to join the rest of the boys. Ryan looked at Mary Kate and gave a short, quick smile. Mary Kate pursed her lips and went back to her reading.

Not too much later, the small berth was crowded with the boys' loud laughter and cigarette smoke, which made it hard for Mary Kate to concentrate on the words.

"Patrick, I'm going up on deck to read!" Mary Kate hopped off the bottom bunk. The boys didn't even notice her leave the room.

Forgetting to take the map with her, Mary Kate was going on memory as to how to find the aft deck. Instead, she went up too many flights of stairs past the second-class promenade to the boat deck. Standing confused on the boat deck for a few seconds, she turned around and smashed right into someone, which sent her book flying on to the deck.

"Whoa!" the young man chuckled. Mary Kate reached down to grab her book, but there were two books on the deck, almost identical. Not wanting to appear foolish, she quickly reached down to snatch up one of the books. But the young man had already picked them both up, and he handed one to Mary Kate. She couldn't help but notice a beautiful gold and ruby ring that adorned his finger. They locked eyes for a moment, then Mary Kate looked away sheepishly.

"I am terribly sorry." She turned red when she saw how good-looking the young man was. Mary Kate never recalled seeing eyes that shade of green.

"No harm done." Matthew brushed himself off, then took a good long look at her. He shivered slightly when he noticed how beautiful she was. Mary Kate smiled and went to move around him, but he stepped in her path, and Mary Kate's stomach twisted in nervous knots.

"My name is M-Matthew Burnes," he stammered nervously, holding his hand out.

"Mary Kate McKinney," Mary Kate said nervously, still trying to get around him, but she took his hand quickly.

"Nice to meet you." Matthew shook her white hand, then tipped his hat. Mary Kate stood there for a few minutes, trying to regain control of herself. She looked down the rail at the deck where she originally wanted to go. Taking a brief look around to see who had witnessed her clumsiness, she then headed down.

Matthew gazed at the young girl, who stood there for a few seconds before disappearing through the door to go to the poop deck. She was beautiful, but she definitely belonged in third class, he could tell by her mismatched clothing and worn shoes.

Pulling a wooden deck lounger into the warm sunshine and lying back, Matthew closed his eyes to the bright sun. He put his book in his lap and debated whether to read or take a nap as he removed his hat. He finally sighed and opened his book.

"Good afternoon, is this lounger taken?" a young woman's voice asked, and Matthew squinted his eyes. His cousin, Virginia, stood before him. The dark feathers in her hat waved in the wind.

"Not at all, Miss, please sit," Matthew said to her playfully as she sat on the lounger next to him daintily.

"Where is David?" Matthew asked his cousin, setting his book under his deck chair and folding his hands in his lap.

"I'm not sure, I haven't seen him since breakfast – oh there he is!" Virginia waved her gloved hand happily at her fiancé, who was striding towards them. She stood up hastily, and David smiled widely, a good-looking young man. The group exchanged pleasantries, and then Matthew was alone again. He sighed and then picked the thick book back up. The words and characters seemed unfamiliar to him. Leaning his head back and taking a deep breath, it dawned on him that he had the wrong book! The breeze picked up and blew open a few pages. A man's face stared back at him from a semi-worn photograph. He picked it up and flipped it over. Matthew considered it none of his business and stuck the photo firmly back in the book. He had to find Miss Mary Kate McKinney and return her book. He dismissed his feelings when his heart leapt in his chest at the thought of seeing her again.

Mary Kate flopped down on a bench on the crowded deck. The bright sunshine helped to warm her in the cool April breeze.

How different the ocean looked in the day compared to the other night, when she watched the stars sparkle and felt the ocean's power. People were scattered on the deck today. Some played games or chatted. Picking up her book and walking over to the rail, Mary Kate leaned over the rail and let the wind take her long auburn curls. She thought she might as well enjoy the ride, because no one knew when she would be back to Europe again. She didn't really even know William, yet he seemed so tense and matter-of-fact in his letters. He kept very tight watch on his pocketbook, that she could tell. He definitely didn't seem like the type who would want to send her home every year, and Mary Kate was used to living poor, so she didn't consider William should spend all his money on her anyway. She would at least be able to help take care of her family by sending money every once in a while. This marriage was a matter of convenience to them both more than it was for love. William wanted an obedient wife, and Mary Kate needed a husband to help her take care of her poor family, her entire reason for doing this.

Mary Kate's Aunt Opal had arranged this whole marriage. Having been born to a poor Irish family herself, Opal had come to America on a filthy, rat-ridden ship some years earlier. Her brother, Mary Kate and Patrick's father, had provided Opal's ticket, but she must fend for herself once in America. When Opal arrived in America, she was hired by a rich Bostonian, whose wife of twenty-seven years died soon after. Opal had always been opportunistic and had taken her chance when it came available. She was known as a gold-digging harlot, and the gossip even went so far as to say as she had poisoned her husband's first wife.

Now Opal had arranged for her niece to marry into the third-richest family in Boston. With empty promises and a lot of encouragement to both sides, William had asked for Mary Kate's hand in marriage. What could Opal's brother do but agree? If he wanted what was best for Mary Kate, he would send her to America. Of course Opal deluded herself that she had Mary Kate's best interests at heart, when all she really wanted to do was link herself to The Richters. Opal had told young William he didn't want any "Boston" girls. They were all so forthright and wanted an education, and there was talk of a "women's movement." She had scared poor William, which was her intention, into picking a young, quiet, and subservient wife. Quickly regaining contact with her family, Opal had told William that her niece would be the perfect choice. Opal hoped her family would come through for her after all the trouble she was putting young William to. Putting the rich to any trouble could spell disaster for Opal's way of life.

Patrick had his own reasons for coming to America. Wanting to get away from a dead-end life in Ireland, he could picture himself working till the day he died, like he knew his father would. Patrick was glad to escort his sister to America, and then he could have a chance to make something of himself.

Mary Kate stepped down off the rail, squinting into the bright yellow sunshine. She heard giggling behind her, which she ignored until she looked up.

"Hi again." It was Matthew! Mary Kate's heart pounded loudly in her chest. Suddenly she felt very nervous. She had never been so embarrassed before by her dress and the patches on the elbows. She folded her arms, ashamed of her appearance. Glancing at a group of girls who sat on a bench by her, Mary Kate saw that they were whispering and giggling quietly. Matthew was very good-looking, and it was evident he was from the first class. Mary Kate silently wondered why he came to a deck that usually only the third-class passengers inhabited.

"Hello," Mary Kate managed to squeak out. Matthew held out the book to her.

"I think I gave you the wrong one." Matthew smiled; he took

27

in Mary Kate's rare beauty. His stomach was full of butterflies as she reached out to take her book.

"Thank you." Mary Kate smiled shyly. Matthew still stood there, and she looked down at her hands, each holding a book.

"Oh!" Mary Kate laughed nervously, then handed Matthew his rightful book. "I didn't even open it yet."

"Oh, that's all right, even if you did. I didn't read yours either, just enough to know it wasn't mine." He thought about the picture he found in her book but decided not to say anything.

"What are you reading?" Mary Kate asked hesitantly.

"Oh, Dickens. *Great Expectations*."

Mary Kate's heart leapt; it was her favorite Dickens novel. "That's a good one. I won't give away the ending but it is good." She smiled, a little more at ease since this was something she knew about. Mary Kate couldn't help but notice Matthew's bright smile that lit up his whole handsome face.

"So you like Dickens? I thought that maybe I was the only one in the whole world. The book you're reading now, is it good?" Matthew pointed to her thick book.

"Yes, pretty good." Mary Kate nodded. "I'll let you borrow it if you like."

Matthew laughed, and he came across as mocking, but actually he was nervous.

"Well, I mean I'm almost done with it, it won't take me long." Mary Kate felt foolish.

"Oh, well, I mean I would hate to take your book. I don't know if I could finish it before we get to New York, I might not be able to locate you to give it back or...."Matthew trailed off. He looked down at his hands, unable to meet her eyes. She definitely was Irish, he could tell by her accent.

"Well, that's all right. Maybe you could get your own copy sometime. Or ... here!" Mary Kate held up the book to Matthew. "Take it as a gift." Matthew's astonishing green eyes widened with surprise. No stranger had just given him anything! Especially anyone with as little to give as this girl.

"No, I couldn't take your book!" Matthew held his hand up.

"Yes, I insist." Mary Kate still held the book out stubbornly.

"No, no I couldn't." Matthew still held stubborn, too.

"Well, how about I give it to you when I'm done? You can really have it."

"No, I shouldn't. I can afford my own copy. Please don't let me take yours," Matthew said somberly. He felt bad when Mary Kate put her arm with her book sadly behind her. He felt he had hurt her feelings, which he didn't mean to do. He certainly wasn't going to make any friends that way, he thought. He couldn't walk away, it seemed a little voice kept whispering to him that there was more to this girl than appeared.

"Listen," he said quietly, "if it means that much to you, I will take it. But normally I don't make a habit of taking things that don't belong to me." Mary Kate smiled, and Matthew instantly felt relief.

The girls behind them had been watching the whole performance and had been giggling the whole time, not unnoticed by Matthew.

"Do you want to go somewhere else?" he asked, pointing away from the stern.

"Maybe we'd better!" Mary Kate whispered as they took off down the deck.

The promenade deck was warm with sunshine. Leaning up against the rail backwards, Matthew smiled at Mary Kate warmly. "Have you ever traveled before?" he asked.

"No, just by foot in our little town in Ireland. Only to go to church really." Mary Kate laughed.

"Let me guess, you are Catholic?" Matthew said sarcastically, his gorgeous eyes danced with friskiness.

"Not all Irish are Catholics." Mary Kate laughed, trying to sound firm.

"Really?" Matthew tried to sound sarcastically surprised.

"Well, no, maybe I'm not Catholic. It's not very nice to judge me like that." Mary Kate was teasing him, but a serious look came over Matthew's face.

"Don't be serious, I was joking you!" She laughed and tugged the arm of his coat playfully. Matthew smiled brightly again, his white teeth all in a straight row.

"Not that you care, but I'm not Catholic." Matthew looked away from her bright azure stare.

Shrugging, Mary Kate leaned her arms on the rail, too. "Makes no difference to me."

The sun was sinking lower in the sky, and she was beginning to feel a slight chill. Matthew noticed this and offered his coat, but she refused. He turned the same direction as Mary Kate was, facing the vast ocean.

"Want to go inside?" He looked at her intently and seriously, and he still couldn't help notice her natural beauty. Her soft demeanor and curly reddish brown hair and glowing white skin. He loved the way she smiled, and he never recalled seeing anyone with eyes so blue.

Opening the door for her, Matthew followed in behind her. Things were suddenly very quiet. There were very few passengers by the grand staircase in the lull before suppertime. Matthew and Mary Kate looked at each other for a moment. Neither one really wanted to part ways as they stood alone near the grand staircase on 'A' deck.

Mary Kate looked up at the glass and black wrought iron dome while Matthew stared at the elevators, hoping someone would come to break the silence.

The clock at the grand staircase began to chime.

Ding … Ding …. Ding … Ding … Ding … Ding…. Not even paying attention to the number of times it chimed, Mary

Kate nervously tapped her toe on the black and white marble floor.

"Do you have to go back?" Matthew finally spoke. The way he stared at her made her feel nervous in an exciting new way.

"Eventually," she spoke quietly, then cleared her throat. She thought she really ought to go back now, or Patrick would worry. She liked Matthew, and she couldn't believe someone as good-looking and polite was so nice to her. The way he looked at her made her tingle inside, yet she didn't want to appear desperate or forward.

"Well...." Matthew was about to say something else.

"Maybe I should just go back." Mary Kate turned to leave.

"What if I don't want you to go?" Matthew blurted out, and Mary Kate looked at him strangely.

"You don't?" she asked, surprised. Matthew shook his head. Mary Kate continued. "I'm not boring you?"

"Of course not! Quite the contrary, but if you have to go...."

"Oh, no, I don't really either," Mary Kate lied, though she knew she should go back to her brother, and Matthew nervously shoved his hands in his brown coat's pockets.

"Well, what should we do now?" he asked, smiling.

"What is there to do?" Mary Kate shrugged.

"I could give you a tour of the grand staircase." Matthew suggested, and Mary Kate smiled in agreement.

The sun had set some time ago. Mary Kate and Matthew had found a cozy spot in the reception room before the first-class dining saloon. The small red velvet and wicker chairs made a comfortable atmosphere for their visit.

"...so actually I'm not traveling alone. I've got my parents' servant with me. He's so sauced, he doesn't know if he's on *Titanic* or a shrimp boat!" Matthew laughed, joking about Thomas.

Mary Kate laughed and sat back in her chair. Today had

been fun, and the last few hours she and Matthew had spent together had been a lot of fun. Her stomach made an awful noise, and she covered it with her hand. Her face turned red, and they both laughed. First-class passengers were starting to head into the dining saloon for supper, staring at the mismatched couple.

"Would you like me to get you something to eat?" Matthew asked, pointing to the dining saloon.

"Oh, no! No!" Mary Kate stood up and pushed the chair in. "I must be going anyway."

Matthew took a step towards her. "I enjoyed today very much, Mary Kate," Matthew said slowly. Using her name made Mary Kate feel uneasy, and she looked away shyly.

"I did as well, thank you for a nice day." Mary Kate shook hands with Matthew, and his touch sent small shivers up her spine. This feeling was new to her, and it warmed her inside. His hand was warm and soft, and she withdrew quickly.

"There you are! I have been looking all over for you!" Patrick's gruff voice broke the moment. He had Sean and Ryan with him.

"Patrick!" Mary Kate turned to face her brother, who stopped dead in his tracks when he saw Matthew. He looked from Mary Kate to Matthew, then back at his sister.

"It is after eight o' clock, Mary Kate. I want you back in the cabin and asleep!" Patrick grabbed her hand roughly and pulled her towards him. His hands were rough and callused compared to Matthew's.

Whatever this man was to Mary Kate, Matthew didn't like the way he treated her, and he stepped forward.

"Patrick," Mary Kate tried to ease the tension, "I'd like you to meet a friend." Easing up a little bit, he let go of his sister's hand, but Patrick still had his eyes fixed on her furiously.

"Matthew Burnes." Matthew smiled his gorgeous smile and extended his hand politely.

"Hi, Patrick McKinney." Patrick shook Matthew's hand roughly, not smiling.

"He's my brother, escorting me to America." Mary Kate turned to Matthew and smiled sweetly. Matthew's heart jumped. Her brother!

"We are going now." Patrick led Mary Kate by the elbow to the elevators, and Ryan, Patrick's friend, shot Matthew an evil glance, his eyes narrowed with bitterness.

Matthew stared after them. It would be a pity if he never saw Mary Kate again; she was beautiful and kind. As he went upstairs and changed into his evening clothes, he wanted to see if he could find his cousin to tell her all about his new friend, Mary Kate.

"Mary Kate, I don't want you to see that boy again!" Patrick inhaled sharply on his cigarette, back in their cabin.

Perhaps Mary Kate was a little afraid of never having Matthew's company again. "Why?"

"He's a no-good first-class snob!" Ryan interjected from across the room.

"It's none of your business, Ryan!" Mary Kate snapped and the boys were shocked at her impoliteness, which was very uncommon for the sweet young woman.

"Mary Kate," Patrick calmly touched her shoulder, "that boy only wants one thing from you. You are already promised to another. William in America." Those words stabbed Mary Kate's heart like a thousand swords. She hadn't thought about William one minute when she was with Matthew.

Ryan stared at her angrily to see what she would say next, while Patrick put his cigarette out in the stool.

"Patrick, I don't like Matthew that way. We have a common interest in books is all," Mary Kate explained to her brother.

"I seen the way you was flirtin' with him!" Ryan stood up and addressed her angrily.

"My sister is right, it is none of your business." Snarling at Ryan, Patrick looked at Mary Kate and raised one furry red eyebrow. Scratching his red moustache thoughtfully, his husky voice was filled with concern.

"I just worry about you, Sis. This is the biggest ship in all the world, and I'm glad you want to make new friends, too. But you have never been out of my sight that long, and I was just worried."

Mary Kate sighed and looked down at her hands with guilt. She looked over at Sean, who had been quiet during this whole time, and he shrugged apologetically.

"I want you all to go away. Go away and leave me alone!" Mary Kate cried, grabbing her book. She flopped on the bottom bunk and buried her face in the parchment pages.

After the boys left the cabin, Mary Kate felt salty tears sting her eyes. They were right! Maybe she was flirting with Matthew. But hadn't he flirted back? Hadn't he shown an interest in her? Mary Kate promised to marry William. The reality of that couldn't stop her from thinking that Matthew was the only boy whose company she actually enjoyed.

Mary Kate cursed herself and told herself to be rational. To forget it. It would never work. In less than a week, she would be in New York to start the life she promised her family she would. The whole entire reason she was on *Titanic* was to go to William, not to be with Matthew.

Mary Kate snapped off the light and rolled under the covers. Would she be able to deny her feelings though? The way her heart jumped when Matthew looked at her or the soft warm touch of his hand on hers or his bright smile that put her at ease? She felt brave at the moment, but when she thought of Matthew's handsome face and the way he smiled at her, her heart melted like hot candle wax under the flame of the wick, and she wasn't sure if she could stay away.

After dinner, Matthew quietly closed the door to the stateroom. Thomas was nowhere around. Having just told Virginia about his new friend, she seemed distant and unwilling to agree about the differences in their status. Virginia told Matthew it was nice to make new friends, but you couldn't decide after one evening if you were in love with someone. Matthew had then carefully pointed out to his cousin how she and David met, and she became defensive and wouldn't talk to Matthew or even meet his eyes. Matthew smiled to himself all the way back to his stateroom. Virginia was so stubborn, and only her cousin could get away with telling her the truth about herself.

Walking into the bathroom, he looked in the shiny mirror at himself. What did Mary Kate see? he wondered. Did she see a handsome young man, or a fool?

Lighting his after-dinner cigarette, the only one he allowed himself a day, Matthew undid his vest and tie. He took off his restrictive shoes and set them neatly under the bed. He stared at the gold and ruby ring on his finger that his father gave to him before he graduated from the university. It was engraved, *Matthew 1911.*

Matthew looked at the ring and saw it in a whole new light, and he was overcome by contempt. His father dared to buy him such gaudy things and underpay and starve his mineworkers. Good, hard-working people, people probably a lot like Mary Kate's family.

Matthew slid the ring off his finger angrily and threw it across the bedroom. It pinged and rattled for a few seconds, and he could care less where it landed. Why did he and Mary Kate have to be of two different worlds? She was beautiful and funny and smart, so who cared if she were poor? He knew that in his heart his parents would never accept her, his mother maybe, definitely not his father. He would lose his inheritance of the mine and have nothing to offer her except more poverty, that she was probably used to. He wanted better than that for her. He cursed himself for thinking about it too much. Mary Kate probably didn't even like him, she probably thought he was dull and arrogant.

Matthew finished undressing and crawled into the fresh white sheets. At least today turned out not to be a loss, he enjoyed talking to Mary Kate, even if nothing else ever happened between them.

Ryan, Sean, and Patrick sat at a planked table playing poker in the third-class general area. People all around of all ages and all races were living it up in the great room. Their one chance to ride on a fantastic and brand new ship.

"Well, I fold!" Ryan threw down his cards with a slap. Patrick raised one fuzzy eyebrow at him, then looked over at Sean.

"Me too." Sean sighed and tossed his cards in front of Patrick.

"Well, I guess I win. Too bad we aren't playin' for money." Patrick chuckled and pulled a cigarette out of his coat pocket.

Ryan stared at Patrick angrily and stomped off after a short "Good night."

"What's with him?" Patrick asked Sean, exhaling his smoke.

"He's got a little problem." Sean said stonily, shuffling the cards.

"Oh? What kind of problem?" Inhaling sharply on his cigarette, Patrick set his brown eyes on his friend and took a gulp of the dark liquid.

Sean couldn't look in Patrick's eyes. "Woman troubles."

"And who might this woman be?" Patrick continued his interrogation. The noise in the room was loud, but Patrick was only interested in what Sean was going to say next.

Sean remained quiet as he continued to shuffle the cards. Patrick was sure his friend heard the question.

"WHO?" he asked again angrily.

Sean looked around nervously before leaning over to Patrick. "Your sister," he whispered hesitantly.

Patrick stood up abruptly and put his hands on the table in front of Sean, blocking him in. "Tell your brother my sister is marrying that American, so he needs to forget about it." Patrick's breath smelled like ale and smoke, and his brown eyes burned with fury.

Sean swallowed hard. Ryan was going to kill him for telling Patrick.

Sean tried to rebut. "Well, I–"

"It's not your fault. But you said what you said – so it must be true. Remember what I said, If he touches my sister, I cannot be responsible for my actions." Patrick shook his finger at Sean, then put his cigarette out in his own beer and stomped away.

Ryan stood inside his cabin, unable to move. He really made a jackass out of himself tonight, but he had been in love with Mary Kate since they were kids. The thought of her going to America to marry some boy she didn't know was bad enough, but now she was flirting with some first-class guy!

Bitter with jealousy and rage, Ryan resolved to think of a way to get her and keep her away from that American boy and that first-class snob. He wanted to have her, and it seemed she paid attention to everyone else but him. The only thing that stopped him was the fact that Patrick would string him up by his toes if Ryan harmed even one hair on Mary Kate's curly head. He knew that Mary Kate could easily be scared into keeping her mouth shut. But what other way to get her for his own than to take her in a way that she would be spoiled for her for her American boy? That would teach her to be a hussy and flirt with strange men on a ship! Ryan put out the light and lay in his bed.

He had to approach her as soon as he could.

Chapter 3

Saturday morning, Mary Kate woke to warm sunlight streaming in through the porthole. She looked out at the endless blue sea as she got dressed in a red plaid skirt and white blouse. She was careful to choose one of her new outfits, that had no patches. She brushed her auburn curls and pulled her hair up loosely. She pulled a black yarn shawl over her shoulders as she passed the looking glass. Before she left, she wondered what Matthew thought of the way she looked. Could it be he just pitied her? Is that why he was nice?

She sighed and headed out the door to breakfast. Patrick had never come back to the cabin last night. Assuming things got late and he slept in Sean and Ryan's cabin, Mary Kate hoped that maybe she could catch him at breakfast.

Mary Kate walked innocently down the passageway when an arm grabbed her and pulled her inside a crew utility room. Ryan harshly pushed her against the white paneled wall as he covered her mouth with his sweaty hand.

"Don't panic!" Ryan said quietly, and he looked around him. He took his hand away from Mary Kate, who stayed up against the wall, her eyes wide, fearing what would happen next.

"What did you do that for?" She finally found courage to speak, her chest heaving and her heart pounding with anxiety.

"I need to tell you somethin'." Ryan put one of his meaty arms out against the wall, blocking Mary Kate in. The way he trapped her made her feel scared.

She stared fearfully at his arm and then at his face. She

stared into his beady brown eyes and noticed the sweat forming on his brow. She folded her arms nervously across her chest. This was unlike him, just as the angry words last night. "What?"

He could feel his anger rise at her dismissal of his feelings. "It's about your first-class little loverboy. I seen him with some girl just last night. They was in the dining room. Him and some hussy just hangin' all over each other," Ryan lied, trying to catch the young woman off guard. She looked away from Ryan's dark stare.

"I told you I don't like him that way," Mary Kate denied, looking at the floor.

Ryan could tell she was lying by the way she couldn't meet his eyes. He fumed and it took all the will power he could muster to stop himself from grabbing her. "FINE!" he yelled at her. "Just when he breaks your heart, don't say I didn't warn you!" Stomping angrily away, Ryan slammed the door shut behind him when he left.

Mary Kate sighed heavily, stunned into stillness for a minute. Should she believe what Ryan told her? She shook off her confusion and headed out of the small room.

Ryan had frightened her so much that she didn't even think to ask where her brother was. She hoped she wouldn't see him again alone, and Mary Kate couldn't figure out why Ryan was so upset about Matthew. He didn't know Matthew or what his intentions were, but those feelings scared her. Maybe her feelings were transparent enough for Ryan to see through them.

People were swaggering in slowly to the dining saloon as Mary Kate stood up from the table. Still no sign of Patrick, and it was impossible to eat after her encounter with Ryan. She wondered where Matthew would be, then chastised herself. She told herself not to be so obvious and flirtatious, and her brother would be so angry with her if she tried to find Matthew on purpose.

Mary Kate stepped out on the poop deck and looked out over the ocean. The wide ocean, with no land in sight, frightened her, but she tried not to think about it. She was on a safe ship, and in no time she would be in America. Her heart dropped when she remembered her reasons for going to America. Mary Kate wished she had brought her book, then she would have something to do. She smiled brightly at a young child passing by and thought that not too long ago, she was that innocent. Now she would have to grow up, and if that meant choosing and making a mature decision, that would be the hardest thing she ever had to do. Her father and brothers usually made all her decisions for her, and Mary Kate trusted them, because she knew they were wise. But what was her heart telling her to do?

Knowing that she shouldn't, Mary Kate went by the grand staircase on her way back to her cabin. She had to find out what her heart was trying to tell her, and it felt as if it would leap out of her chest when she spied Matthew sitting in a chair reading a book. His back was turned to her, and when she looked at him, she knew what Ryan said couldn't be true. It didn't even enter her mind or deter her from wanting to talk to him.

Hearing heels clicking on the marble floor behind him, Matthew looked up from his book, then turned his attention back to his reading. His heart leapt wildly when he realized whom he just recognized!

"Good morning." Mary Kate smiled shyly, her hands clasped behind her back.

"Good morning yourself!" Matthew smiled and leapt out of his chair and hurried over to her. He still couldn't believe how his heart leapt every time he looked at her.

"I was going to come and see if I could find you. How are you?" Matthew asked.

"What? Oh, fine … I mean." Mary Kate laughed nervously; she had forgotten how handsome he was.

"Good…." Matthew stood staring at her for a few seconds, not sure what to say next.

Mary Kate forgot all about her encounter with Ryan when Matthew was so near. She looked at her hands guiltily when she thought about having to tell Matthew about her reason for going to America.

"Can we take a walk instead of just standing here?"

"Matthew, don't you think people talk about us … when we're together?" Mary Kate asked anxiously. She wanted to know what he was thinking about their differences in status.

"I don't care what people say. We're both paying passengers on this ship, and we can do as we please," Matthew said matter-of-factly. Mary Kate's heart started pounding again, and she thought she should will it to stop for fear Matthew would hear it.

She asked hesitantly. "You aren't afraid to be seen with me?"

Matthew shook his head and reached for her hand. Mary Kate looked down at the two of their hands clasped together, and she liked the feel of his warm, soft hand holding hers.She withdrew her hand timidly and smiled up at Matthew.

"Should we walk then?" she asked. Matthew smiled and offered his elbow to escort her. Mary Kate chuckled softly. Being with Matthew was fun, and it made her happy. So why should she deny her feelings? *For my family*, Mary Kate thought, and her heart sank to the bottom of her stomach again. She would have to tell him about William and America today.

The cool ocean breeze flew past Mary Kate and Matthew on the promenade deck. Matthew leaned up on the rail backward to face her. "Do you know it takes almost ten days to cross the Atlantic on a regular steamer?" Matthew pointed westward in the direction the ship was steaming.

Mary Kate smiled, listening intently. "You sound like quite the sailor!" she chided.

"Oh, I've been back and forth a few times to go home for holidays and what not."

"So how long does it take *Titanic* to cross?" she queried.

"She's never made the trip across, so I guess we'll find out." Matthew smiled, and his green eyes twinkled. Mary Kate had not noticed the brown specks that danced inside of the green.

Mary Kate thought briefly about her encounter with the Englishman and his prediction of disaster for the ship. She didn't tell Matthew for fear he would think she was as crazy as the Englishman. "If she gets into New York by Thursday or Friday, I'll be happy." Mary Kate folded her arms across her chest as the sun reached the top of the azure sky.

"Why, what's waiting for you in New York?" Matthew asked innocently, squinting into the cold sunshine. Mary Kate felt a twinge of pain. Now was the perfect time to tell the truth, but she couldn't do it.

"Oh, all sorts of things, but nothing as exciting as you." Mary Kate tried to change the subject.

"I don't want to talk about me. You must be going to America for some reason?"

"Please don't pry, Matthew. I can't tell you, not now," Mary Kate whispered. The air became tense between them.

"I'd better go back, my brother is probably looking for me." Mary Kate gestured towards the stern of the ship.

Matthew looked at her seriously. "Must you go? I suppose your brother is mad at me?"

"No, he's mad at me. I frightened him by being gone so long yesterday." Mary Kate couldn't meet Matthew's eyes, and he silently nodded. The sun beat down on them as a heavy silence fell like an anchor.

"Can I come with you?" Matthew asked her bravely.

"Down to third class?" Mary Kate was mortified at the thought of the look on her brother's face if he saw Matthew with her below deck.

"Sorry! I thought first-class people were snobs, not third class!" Matthew laughed.

Mary Kate giggled nervously. "I'm sorry, Matthew. But I don't think the captain wants us to mix class."

"I could pretend like I didn't know that!"

"I think they would know a man of your upbringing would know better!" Mary Kate laughed under her breath.

The pair fell silent for a moment, both excited and nervous at the same time.

"So, when can I be with you again?" Matthew asked her out of the blue, and Mary Kate gave him a strange look.

"What?"

"Can't you join me for supper tonight?"

"Are you still talking to me?" She pointed her finger at herself in disbelief.

"No, I'm talking to the lady standing behind you. Of course I'm talking to you!" Matthew joked.

Believing her ears were deceiving her, Mary Kate trembled. "So you think they do Irish jigs in first class now?"

"We don't have to dance, but we can if you want," Matthew said nervously.

"Yes, I'm sure we would be the hit of the dance floor." Mary Kate laughed nervously. Her heart was bursting with happiness, yet afraid of the consequences if she disobeyed her brother.

"I am serious, and you are going to hurt my feelings," Matthew said somberly.

Mary Kate looked him in his serious eyes and thought a minute before speaking. "But Matthew, I have nothing to wear, and I don't know how to fashion my hair like fancy people or–"

"Poppycock! My cousin, Virginia, is on board, and if I know her, she will have something you can wear. Please! I won't take no for an answer," Matthew pleaded.

"All right!" Mary Kate finally agreed to meet him at eight o'clock at the grand staircase.

Patrick's head was throbbing. He had gotten a little wild last night and fallen asleep in a stoker's room. Later that afternoon, Mary Kate was nowhere to be seen. He looked in all the third-class general areas but was unable to find her. He ran into his friend Sean in the passageway.

"Have you seen Mary Kate?" Patrick asked Sean with a hoarse voice, grabbing on to Sean's jacket for support.

"I was just goin' to ask ya if ya seen Ryan!" Sean said tensely, just as Ryan came charging down the hall.

"Jesus, Brother! Where ya been all day?" Sean ran over to him, but Ryan said nothing.

"Ryan, have you seen Mary Kate?" Patrick asked frantically.

"Yeah, you could say that. I saw her this mornin', but not since," Ryan said angrily.

"What is that supposed to mean?"

"Well, what do *you* think?" Ryan was pushing Patrick's limits.

"She wouldn't! Mary Kate is a good girl, and she knows better than that!" Patrick was seething.

Sean gave his brother an enough-is-enough look and hauled him down the corridor.

She wouldn't, Patrick thought angrily.

Mary Kate pretended to be reading quietly when Patrick entered the room. He tossed his brown coat on the top bunk and lit a cigarette. "Where you been hidin' all day?" Smoke filled up the small room as Patrick questioned his sister gruffly.

Mary Kate sat up slowly. "Around."

"You have managed to evade me."

Mary Kate pursed her lips and looked away from his eyes. She couldn't lie to her brother, especially when her cheeks were burning red.

"Damn it, woman!" Patrick slammed his cigarette in the commode.

"Patrick, you don't understand!" Mary Kate stood up and moved towards her brother.

"I think I understand very clearly!" Wailing in a high-pitched voice, Patrick turned away from his sister.

"No, Patrick, it's not like that!"

"You are a shameless hussy! You are marrying someone else already, by God! I'm taking you to America to marry him! Forever is a long time when you've made a promise, and you've made a promise!" Patrick had a bad temper but had never directed it towards his sister before.

"Patrick, I-I-I don't know what to say!" Mary Kate stuttered, and her blue eyes glistened with tears. Patrick softened a little and took his little sister by her shoulders and he locked his eyes with hers.

"You have got to tell that boy good-bye, Mary Kate. It's not fair to lead him on. It's not fair, because he can't love you. His parents will not allow him to marry a poor Irish girl." What her brother said was making sense, but it did not deter Mary Kate. She had promised Matthew she would meet him tonight, even if it were to say good-bye.

Matthew whistled happily as he continued to walk along the deck down to the stern. The last couple of days had all happened so suddenly, but he couldn't deny what he felt in his heart. Meaning to express himself fully to Mary Kate tonight, he felt nervous but sure of his feelings.

Matthew had given a lot of thought to what was going to happen when he told his parents. He planned to wire ahead so that they could be prepared, but it made no difference to the young man, because he was sure of his feelings, no matter what his parents would say or do.

Watching him with jealous eyes from a bench, Ryan was consumed with rage. He knew it was that American boy that Mary Kate had disappeared with. *Curse him and his good looks and charm!* Ryan would beat him down now if the deck weren't so populated.

Even harder to bear was the young man's happy smile and his perky whistling. It brought Ryan's blood to a boil, since he knew the reason for the young man's good mood must be that he had just seen the young and beautiful Mary Kate.

Matthew walked up to the very back of the stern and leaned over the rail to look at the massive wake that the propellers kicked up. A larger man approached Matthew and tapped him on the shoulder.

Ryan watched with interest as the men conversed shortly, and he thought he had seen the round, older man before in the third-class saloon. The young American's expression turned from curiosity to annoyance as he reached in his pants pocket and withdrew some paper currency that he then handed over.

As the fatter man walked away, Ryan realized that they must have somehow been traveling together. He leaned forward on the bench, watching the scenario. He had to find a way to get this boy out of the picture, and the fat man just might just be the key to the door.

Chapter 4

Mary Kate squinted at the piece of White Star Line stationery in one hand and Patrick's wrinkly map of the ship in the other. The number of the room where Matthew said his cousin would be was etched on the stationery in pencil. B-66. Mary Kate stood in front of the white door and knocked hesitantly. She sighed and looked around her, hoping no one saw her.

The door opened abruptly, and there stood the most beautiful girl Mary Kate had ever seen. Like a princess from a fairy tale, her eyes were a fiery green, and her hair was dark brown, nearly black. The girl smiled immediately and grabbed Mary Kate's hand.

Virginia smiled coyly. "So you must be Mary Kate."

"Yes, you must be Virginia." Mary Kate smiled back nervously.

"Matthew has told me a lot about you." Virginia smiled mischievously, going to the wardrobe and pulling out a colorful array of dresses. She tossed the clothes on the bed and continued to talk.

Mary Kate looked around in astonishment at the posh room. The furniture was velvety and smooth, and the fireplace trim was made of the warmest wood she had ever seen. The blue brocaded wallpaper shimmered in the setting sun.

"Matthew can't say that much about me, he hasn't known me but for a day." Mary Kate finally laughed in response.

Virginia said slyly, "Oh, trust me, Mary Kate, Matthew has plenty to say about you."

Mary Kate's cheeks flushed while Virginia busied herself arranging things on the bed.

"Now, Mary Kate, I'll let you pick which you like best. Then we'll see about getting you dressed. I usually have a maid, but this trip was sort of *unexpected.*" Virginia searched Mary Kate's expression. The poor thing was so shy and not used to attention, obviously, but she knew her cousin was mad about this girl. He had never been so fascinated with any woman before, and at first it was hard for Virginia to give in to the idea, yet she pondered lightly what would happen when the ship docked.

Mary Kate walked around the bed slowly and looked at all the beautiful dresses lying there. There was a rainbow of colors before her perplexed eyes. Mary Kate kept looking, reminiscing about the ladies she had seen when they set sail.

"They are all so beautiful, Virginia, how do I pick?" Mary Kate held up her arms and shrugged.

Virginia laughed and came over to stand by her. "Well, let's start with the colors that look good on you." Virginia held each one of the dresses up to Mary Kate's creamy complexion. Three dresses remained on the bed when she was through.

"Now, we find what kind of mood you're in to make the final decision." Virginia held up the red, "Sexy?" She asked, and Mary Kate laughed and covered her mouth with her hand. Virginia laughed, too, at the idea of this shy girl suddenly becoming a sexy society princess.

"All right, no, serious?" Virginia asked in a low tone, holding up a dark blue dress. Mary Kate shook her head. Virginia tossed it to the side, too.

"Well, this is the last one left, it will have to do!" Virginia held up the dark green velvet gown. It had a square neckline and empire waist, with crème-colored lace at the elbow-length sleeves. Not too fancy, but Virginia figured that without all the regular frippery of dinner dresses of the day, it would be just right for Mary Kate.

Virginia helped Mary Kate get into a corset, and the young Irish woman, who had never seen such a contraption, was stunned at the tightness of it.

"Do you always have to wear these things?" Mary Kate gasped, hanging on to the bedpost.

"Most of the time, yes, or the dress won't fit properly." Virginia continued cinching it.

"I almost can't breathe." Mary Kate laughed, and Virginia giggled.

"Well, let the voice of experience tell you not to make any sudden moves either, or you will cut your breast in half!" Virginia laughed.

Mary Kate laughed louder than she thought she ever had before, such talk! "It hurts to laugh, too," Mary Kate sighed with a smile.

"Well, I'm just about done." Virginia tied the final knot and pulled the green dress off the hanger. She slipped the sheet of green velvet over Mary Kate's head and adjusted it so the dress would hang correctly.

"Go look in the mirror before we start on your hair." Virginia smiled and started to pick up the mess of dresses scattered about before doing Mary Kate's finishing touches.

Mary Kate couldn't believe she was looking at herself in the mirror. She was beautiful in that gown. It twirled and swirled, and it flowed so gracefully. She was sure if her father could see her, he would not approve of this! The pangs of guilt tugged at her heart, but not for long.

Virginia watched Mary Kate look at herself in the mirror. Mary Kate was so young and full of hope, and Virginia secretly hoped Matthew had thought about this. Mary Kate was so beautiful, naturally, and certainly she could have any man if she set her mind to it. The only thing holding her back was her shyness. There were also the differences in status to worry about. Virginia knew her aunt and uncle would not be ready to accept Mary Kate with open arms. Her uncle, yes, in time. Her aunt, never! Virginia wondered if Matthew had also thought of this.

Virginia brought a chair over to the mirror and pushed Mary Kate into it. She took apart Mary Kate's bun and began gently combing through her dark auburn curls.

"What beautiful hair!" Virginia smiled at Mary Kate in the mirror.

Mary Kate smirked. "Thank you!"

Virginia pulled Mary Kate's hair in a loose pile on top of her head and stuck a comb with pearls in it to hold it up. Loose curls fell around Mary Kate's face and neck, and Virginia put a small pearl choker around Mary Kate's pretty neck. Virginia gave her a little bit of lipstick, handed her a little pair of crème gloves, and squirted her several times with a flowery musk perfume.

"Look at you now, just like Cinderella!" Virginia smiled and then hugged Mary Kate.

"I'm sorry, I just can't believe all your kindness!" Mary Kate smiled, and Virginia handed her a handkerchief that matched the beautiful lace on her borrowed dress.

"I think the world of you, because my cousin thinks the world of you. He asked me to do this, and I just couldn't say no. You are welcome with me anytime, Mary Kate." The girls hugged, and Mary Kate promised to return Virginia's things right after church in the morning.

Standing in the shiny narrow passageway outside Virginia's room, Mary Kate touched her hair to make sure it was still in place. Two ladies were exiting the elevator, dressed for dinner. One lady, as they passed by Mary Kate, looked the young woman over from one end to the other and gave her an evil snobbish glare.

Mary Kate looked away, flushing. That lady didn't know Mary Kate, and yet, she saw right through her. That lady knew Mary Kate didn't belong with 'them'. Mary Kate's heart started to feel heavy. How could she ever think this would be a good idea? Everyone would know she wasn't part of their clique, because she was just a poor Irish girl, just like Patrick had told her. She belonged below decks with others of 'her' kind. She should go back to her cabin and go to bed. She would trade clothes in the morning with Virginia like the girls had originally planned and get her old clothes back in the morning; clothes that seemed so dingy and dirty compared to the ones she stood in now. Mary Kate decided she must tell Matthew anyway, and she headed for the grand staircase.

Matthew waited anxiously at the reception room to the first-class dining saloon. The dining room was ablaze with light and laughter and the sound of voices making idle chatter. Crystal and china clinked and clanked busily as people took their turns eating and visiting on this ship, as grand as any fine hotel.

Looking down at his black patent feet, Matthew stood with his manicured hands clasped in front of him. He tapped his left foot nervously on the black-and-white marble floor as he heard the band warming up nearby.

Mary Kate felt more nervous than she ever had before. She descended the grand staircase slowly, past the clock. The clock Matthew showed her yesterday during their staircase tour. "Honor and Glory Crowning Time." It looked to her like two angels holding a clock before Matthew told her its significance and its meaning. The way he explained it to her made her feel deeply respectful of this intelligent man. He knew so much, why in the world would he want to be with her, a poor, dumb Irish girl?

Mary Kate's breath left her as the clock began to chime eight. The eight chimes sounded like eight warnings. Go back

… Go back … Go back. She saw Matthew waiting at the bottom of the stairs. He was talking to another gentleman now, but Mary Kate froze by the banister, breathing shallow. She felt herself staring at Matthew, so handsome in his tails and dress attire.

Noticing the same ladies that walked by her in the hallway, Mary Kate snapped back to reality. She turned and ran back up the staircase, hoping Matthew hadn't seen her. How hard it was to run with the cumbersome corset, and the borrowed velvet dress deafened her ears as it rustled all the way up the stairs.

Tears flooded her eyes as she burst out the door onto the boat deck. The sky was black, and the stars twinkled like diamonds as the cool ocean breeze dried the tears spilling from her blue eyes.

Virginia told her she was like Cinderella. If she were, where was her Fairy Godmother? *Come rescue me!* Mary Kate pleaded silently. She flopped down on a wooden bench, her face in her hands.

Matthew looked at the clock. Eight twenty. Did she forget? Maybe her brother was forbidding her from coming.

"Coming to eat, dear?" Virginia passed by, a worried look on her face.

Matthew grabbed his cousin's elbow and pulled her aside. "Did she come to find a dress?" he asked frantically.

Virginia nodded; her jeweled earrings clanking in accord.

Matthew rolled his eyes and sighed. Maybe Mary Kate changed her mind, and she didn't want to be with him but she couldn't even do him the favor of telling him?

"She hasn't come yet?" Virginia asked, worried.

"Would I be asking otherwise?"

Virginia could see Matthew was upset.

"I'm sure she'll be along soon." Virginia smiled and tried to comfort her cousin, but he looked at the floor, nodding and not smiling. Promising she would check up on Matthew later, Virginia scurried away to find her fiancé, David, first.

Taking another look around the first-class dining area, a lump formed in Matthew's throat. Deep down, he knew she wasn't coming, but he resolved to go find her. If she didn't want him, she would have to tell him to his face.

Making his way into steerage, Matthew didn't care about the snickers and stares directed at the first-class man all decked out in tuxedo, roaming around the third-class areas. He searched every passageway he could find. Yesterday, Mary Kate tried to explain which cabin was hers, but he sensed that she didn't know her way around very well, and he soon gave up on her directions.

Matthew went down a few stairs into the third-class general area, where a party was beginning to get underway. He saw Thomas, his butler, sitting with a couple of young guys, swilling a bottle. Matthew chortled, *how typical*, he thought. He saw Mary Kate's brother, and the two men locked eyes for a moment. Patrick couldn't move. He hitched up his trousers and looked away from Matthew's stare.

Damn! Matthew thought. If she hadn't told her brother about their dinner plans tonight, Patrick would definitely suspect something now. Matthew saw a few girls that were similarly dressed to Mary Kate, but none could compare to her beauty. He resolved to find her, even if he had to search every inch of the ship!

Angrily slamming the door open to the boat deck, Matthew cursed to himself quietly as he walked along by the palm court.

Mary Kate sat upright on the bench with wide eyes. Matthew froze. He could tell she had been crying, and he leaned up backwards on the rail. He lit a cigarette and avoided her gaze.

"You are mad at me, aren't you?" Mary Kate asked quietly. The sad melody that wafted out of the windows in the palm court provided a match for their feelings. The red glow of Matthew's cigarette was the only light.

"I didn't say that." Matthew turned away from her to face the ocean. They could hear the sound of the wake the huge ship left behind it in the black ocean as it steamed westward.

Mary Kate looked at her feet and sighed. Her head hurt from crying, and she rubbed her temple. "You should be. I'm sorry!" Mary Kate muttered through her tears.

Matthew could only stare at her and wonder what was so upsetting. "If you didn't like me and didn't want to be with me, then why didn't you just say so?" Matthew tossed his cigarette over the side of the ship, then turned to look Mary Kate in the eye, expecting a reply.

"You don't understand." Mary Kate choked. "I don't belong with you. I like you very much, Matthew." Mary Kate wiped her nose on the dainty handkerchief she had borrowed from Virginia.

"I already told you that I don't care if you're not some rich princess! As a matter of fact, that would be a big deterrent." Matthew leaned forward, his arms outstretched.

Mary Kate stared at him and swallowed hard. She should tell him about William, but she just couldn't do it! "I do like you very much, Matthew, you would have to believe that, or else I wouldn't be crying!"

"Then prove it to me, Mary Kate! Because right now, I don't know! I feel like you left me stranded. I've never felt so lost or disappointed, and it's got to be you. I just … I just want to be with you!" Matthew pleaded, and Mary Kate could tell he was struggling to find the right words.

Mary Kate stared at him, shocked. She really couldn't believe he liked her that much. Did this good-looking smart man really want her? She realized suddenly that she had never been so self-conscious about herself until Matthew appeared in her life. Why did she think he was better than she was? Weren't they both human? Did class really matter to him? She shook her head as if to dispel all the questions coming to her mind. She stared at his handsome face. He really did want to be with her! Her heart had been telling her what to do this whole time! Now Mary Kate felt as if her heart could grow wings and fly away. She understood now why she felt so emotional. She really needed to know if Matthew was for real, and he was!

Standing up and walking over to Matthew, Mary Kate touched his hand softly as he wrapped his arm around her waist. "I'm sorry, Matthew, I didn't mean to hurt you." Mary Kate went on to explain about the ladies in the passageway. She continued sadly, shaking her head, "I can only hold you back."

"What can I do to make you understand that I don't care?" he replied in a whisper.

Mary Kate sniffled and pulled away from his grasp. She dreaded ever having to tell Matthew about William. "Well, it's not so easy."

"I cannot figure you out!" Matthew laughed sarcastically and threw his hands up in the air.

Mary Kate smiled coyly and looked away.

"What more do I have to do? Do you want me to get down on one knee?" Matthew knelt down and took her gloved hand.

"Stop it!" Mary Kate looked around nervously and tried to pull away from him.

"What, isn't this good enough? Isn't this what you want?"

Mary Kate felt bad, like he was mocking her. "Stop! Please!" she pleaded, fearing someone in the palm court would see or hear them.

Matthew stood up and put his hands on Mary Kate's shoulders. She had to tell him about William, but her courage left her when Matthew was near.

"What then do I have to do?" His eyes searched hers for an answer. They stood silent for several minutes as Matthew gazed at her longingly. She looked more beautiful than any first-class woman he had ever seen. Even with her eyes red and glossy from crying, she exuded beauty and love from her every pore.

A new tune flowed out of the palm court windows, and Matthew's eyes lit up. Mary Kate was about to say something.

"When all else fails, dance!" Matthew interrupted her, and he pulled Mary Kate further up the deck where there was a little more space to move.

"I can't dance!"

"That's just an excuse, c'mon, I'll lead you!"

"Oh!" Mary Kate gasped as Matthew pulled her close to his body and began to move her in circles. His hand was warm as he pressed it into the small of her back, pushing her ever closer to him. Her heart pounded as their legs moved in rhythmic tandem. This was as close as she had ever been to a man that wasn't her father or brother. How good it felt to dance, though! Swaying softly to the music, she began to smile. Her smile finally burst forth into giggles like a shaken bottle of champagne exploding.

"See, it is fun!" Matthew laughed with her.

The whole world melted away as the pair continued to move to the music together.

Mary Kate never felt so close to anyone, and how could she not notice how close her and Matthew's bodies were? Soon they got carried away, and Mary Kate accidentally stepped on Matthew's foot.

"Ow!" Matthew howled.

Mary Kate giggled nervously. "Sorry!"

The song ended, and the couple stood there silently, still in each other's arms. Each wondered what was going to happen next. Matthew leaned his head down, his handsome clean-shaven face coming closer to Mary Kate's. Her breath quickened. The sea breeze flew around them, blowing Mary Kate's auburn curls around her face. Was he going to kiss her? Her whole body tingled and ached. She couldn't describe the feeling, because it was new to her, but it was a yearning she never knew she was capable of until tonight. Matthew held her so close. He smelled so clean and manly it made her feverish.

Suddenly, the door to the boat deck burst open, and a drunken older couple came out on deck, laughing. Mary Kate and Matthew broke apart quickly; both a little embarrassed about the kiss they almost shared.

"I'd better go." Mary Kate smiled nervously, fussing with her hair.

"You always want to go when I'm having fun!" Matthew teased her, then he insisted she let him walk her back to her cabin, since it was getting late.

Matthew led Mary Kate to the end of the corridor to her cabin, his hand protectively on her back the entire way. She was sure she could find the cabin herself this time, but before she headed down the hall, she and Matthew looked at each other for a lingering moment.

"Well, good-bye." Matthew reached out his hand to her. Mary Kate looked into Matthew's piercing green eyes, then looked at his hand and took it, smiling. She thought to herself that it was a shame she still had her gloves on and couldn't feel the warm skin of his hands.

"Good-bye." Mary Kate wanted to ask if they could meet tomorrow, but she had better leave it at good-bye. They let go of their handshake reluctantly.

"I really enjoy your company, and I would like to see you tomorrow." Matthew said what she hoped he would.

"Well, mass is at noon. You know us Catholics." They both laughed nervously.

"How about after that?" Matthew looked at her longingly.

Mary Kate nodded and smiled. Then she waved her hand and gave Matthew one last glance over her shoulder, and they both waved again before she disappeared out of sight.

Mary Kate closed the cabin door and locked it. Thank God

Patrick wasn't back yet! First thing after church, Mary Kate would return Virginia's things and thank her. Perhaps someday Mary Kate would be able to return the favor.

Mary Kate wrestled with the corset to get it off; her arms were fatigued along with the rest of her by the time she got it off.

The Catholic mass was held at noon on the great liner, so Mary Kate decided she had better get to bed. It must be nearly midnight! She snapped the light back on after a few minutes. How could she sleep? Matthew was in love with her, she knew it for sure now. He twirled her and nearly kissed her! Blood coursed through her veins at the thought of their near-kiss. Stroking the green velvet dress that she now hid under her bedcovers, Mary Kate remembered what the dress felt like on her skin and what it felt like for Matthew to touch her when they danced.

Mary Kate smiled and rolled over on her bed to turn the light back out, when her book fell on the floor. The picture of William scattered out, face up. Her heart leapt involuntarily with anguished guilt. His stern face stared back at her from the photograph. Almost as if he knew. Mary Kate picked up the picture and sighed. William knew she was coming to America. William didn't know Matthew or that Mary Kate was falling in love with him! What would she do when she got to America?

Mary Kate shut out the light and slept on and off for almost an hour, when the doorknob jiggled. Patrick entered the room, and Mary Kate sat up and turned the light on again. Patrick saw his sister was awake and sat down on the edge of the bottom bunk, where Mary Kate remained motionless. He smelled awful, like cheap beer and smoke.

"Mary Kate, your heart hurts, doesn't it?" Patrick hiccuped, his hand on his left breast. Mary Kate sniffled and nodded her head.

Patrick pulled his little sister close to him. "There. There."

He didn't know what to say. A couple of days ago she was his innocent little sister, and now she was wild with love.

After a few minutes, Patrick lifted Mary Kate's chin with his hand to look in her cool blue eyes.

"What are you going to do?" he asked her solemnly.

"Patrick, I just don't know!" Mary Kate looked away from her brother's gaze.

"I know this is hard for you, but do you remember what I said? He can't have you. I could tell that Richter boy that you fell off the ship and you could go with that first-class fella, but Mary Kate, even if you went with him, his family would disown him. He brings home a poor Irish girl?" Patrick shook his head with a look of disgust on his face.

Mary Kate leaned over into her brother's strong shoulder; his dark rough hands held her soft white ones.

"Patrick, it wasn't easy." Mary Kate's tears spilled quietly over her rosy cheeks. Patrick patted her soft hair. "I mean, Patrick, I'm going to marry William Richter. I will go tomorrow to tell Matthew good-bye. You are right, I should never have led him to believe there was any chance. I'm sorry if I doubted you."

Patrick smiled wearily at his sister, he knew she could have any man. He still wasn't sure if she were making the right decision. He pitied her anyway, having to choose like that. Some are never lucky enough to get to choose their love. He blamed himself, he should have just kept her below deck, and she never would have met Matthew then. But would her life be better now because she had met Matthew? Was Matthew the right one for Mary Kate? Were they meant to be together? Patrick pondered silently.

"Mary Kate, I think you are doing the right thing. I've been meaning to talk to you anyway." Patrick's voice became very serious now. "It seems Ryan is in love with you, too." Mary Kate's heart pounded furiously when she realized that must be the reason why Ryan cornered her in the utility room. "He's to the point where he would stop at nothing to get you, like a crazed animal or something," Patrick continued.

Mary Kate swallowed hard and tried to concentrate on her brother's words. "I will be careful," she replied to her brother's warning. How could she have been so naïve?

The siblings kissed good night, and Mary Kate snuggled in her fresh covers. She was exhausted from this day and it's range of emotion.

"And by the way," Patrick said from the top bunk, "wash that hussy-smellin' perfume off before mass tomorrow!" Mary Kate smiled quietly to herself, and the light clicked off for the last time that night.

Thomas sat at the table, swilling the bottle of scotch up to his mouth. He was getting numb, and what better way to spend a vacation that was on the Burnes? He resented having to be their babysitter. *Damn bastard, why can't he go get his own son?* Thomas was secretly angry the day that Mr. Burnes had asked him to retrieve Matthew from Europe.

Thomas looked around at the people on this ship. They sure could live it up! These people knew how to live, and the decadent man could easily disappear among them. The table he sat at had a few men playing cards and smoking.

"Do you want to be in on this round?" a strange young man asked him.

"Well ... sure ... that would be ... wonderful!" Thomas blathered, the scotch beginning to affect him greatly.

Thomas played cards for a great while, oblivious to the fact that someone behind him had pick-pocketed all his money. He decided to fold his hand and bumped his bottle of scotch. It spilled all over the table, and everyone else jumped up to avoid getting wet.

"Oh, shit!" Thomas mumbled through his rotted teeth and

picked up the bottle, the whole thing had damn near been emptied with its spill.

"Listen, friend, if you tell me about your first-class friend you're travelin' with, I'll give you a new damn bottle!" a strange young man approached him.

Thomas eyed the young man that had just spoken to him. "Why do you need to know?" Thomas swilled what was left out of the tall scotch bottle.

"I saw you with your little master the other day. I've seen your master before though."

Thomas thought he should make this little scurvy brat pay him up in drinks before he started talking. "Oh you have?"

"Yes, I think I seen him with some little third-class girl."

"So? My master likes girls, that ain't no surprise!" Thomas laughed, his British accent sounding slurred with drink.

"Well, I happen to like this girl, too." The dark-haired young man looked around to see who was listening, but everyone else seemed occupied.

"So what? You want me to tell the little bastard to stay away from her?" Thomas chuckled at something that he knew he would never have the courage to actually do.

"Well, I think we could work something out." The young man began to give a little more information to Thomas, and soon Thomas' ears started to burn with comprehension. Maybe he could find a way to get back at the Burnes!

Chapter 5

Matthew fixed his collar and bow tie as he got ready for service Sunday morning. There was going to be a general church service in the first-class dining saloon for all classes that morning.

Thomas burped crudely and was chewing mints to try to get the alcohol off his breath before the service. Matthew shook his head in disgust. As far as he was concerned, Thomas should have just stayed passed out.

"You know.... You haven't done a damn thing since we boarded this ship," Matthew said, still adjusting his clothing in the mirror.

Thomas sighed and settled in against the back of the couch. "Well, if you don't mind, Master Burnes, I'm enjoying a little free time away from your parents."

Matthew turned and stared sharply at Thomas. He stopped fiddling with his clothes for a moment and let his arms drop to his side. "Well, Thomas, I don't really want you here, if you must know the truth, you are here because my parents thought I needed a nanny." Matthew seethed and stomped off into the lavatory.

Thomas felt resentment towards Matthew and the entire Burnes family rise to his throat, and he swallowed hard. He had worked hard for many years for this family, and now he was being made a fool by that spoiled little nit-wit! Almost laughing to himself, Thomas knew of the revenge that would befall his master soon.

Mary Kate and Patrick sat in mass in the second-class dining area shortly after noon on Sunday. Mary Kate smiled over at her brother, a new sense of peace between them.

"...go in peace to love and serve the Lord," Father Byles finished as everyone chorused "Amen" and commenced to sing "*Amazing Grace.*"

Mary Kate stood up from kneeling and made the sign of the cross. She pulled her black yarn shawl around her shoulders and turned to leave, catching sight of Ryan and Sean. Sean smiled happily and waved, obviously unaware of his brother's actions yesterday. Ryan looked at Mary Kate, and instead of the angry look that she expected, he gave her a smile and short bow. Looking away in haste, Mary Kate held on to her brother's strong arm as they exited the saloon.

Patrick smiled warmly at his sister. The sun shone brightly through porthole windows as it bathed the floor near where they stood and warmed the inside of the ship. The windows were so fresh and clean, just like everything else on the ship that was so brand new.

"Do you need to go?" Patrick asked his sister, he knew what she must do.

Mary Kate nodded weakly. She felt as if she could cry again, and she looked over at her brother for strength.

Putting on his brown fez cap and adjusting it, Patrick buttoned up his wool brown coat and stretched his rough hand out to his sister, but he couldn't meet her eyes. "I will go with you if you want," he offered.

Mary Kate removed her white headscarf, and wiry tendrils of auburn curls came loose with it. She handed the scarf to her brother. "I would like to go alone, please take this back to the cabin for me," Mary Kate stated blankly with sad eyes.

Patrick watched her walk up the stairs to ascend to the next deck level, all the while cursing himself silently. His heart told him that she was making a mistake by telling Matthew good-bye, but he couldn't stop her, because she had to do what was right. Mary Kate was a good girl, and she would do what she promised her family. Patrick was now convinced that she was committing herself to a life of hell with that Richter boy. Running halfway up the stairs to retrieve her, he knew he should tell her that she best do what her heart told her, but he stopped and stood stunned on the stairs.

Tears stung Patrick's brown eyes, and he removed his cap and slapped it against his leg. He ran back to his cabin to avoid anyone seeing him with wet eyes. Was it so bad just to want what was best for his sister?

Matthew walked into the small office and knocked on the already open door. The last words he heard were "another ice warning." The two young men looked up at him, and the one looked like he had just seen a ghost. All three men just stared at each other for a brief moment.

"Well, get on with it, go tell the captain." The one sitting in the chair rushed the younger man out the door. He gave Matthew a strange look as he passed him in the doorway.

"I was wondering if I could send a telegram?" Matthew asked. The man sitting nodded and took Matthew's information.

Matthew walked out of the telegraph office and up to the boat deck. The warm sunshine beat down on him and he felt so warm, inside and out. He leaned over the rail and took a deep breath of the fresh April air. Last night, dancing with Mary Kate, had been the best time of his life. He hummed to himself the tune they had danced to last night. He remembered the way her perfume smelled and the way her soft skin felt. He thought about the near-kiss they shared, and it made him shiver.

Resolved that he was going to marry her, Matthew knew he

would lose his inheritance, but he knew he could work hard and earn them a living. If he had to live without her, his inheritance wouldn't be worth it. Matthew was filled with hope as he continued his walk down the boat deck.

Matthew looked up and stopped dead in his tracks. Mary Kate stood there, breathtakingly beautiful in a blue dress. Her auburn hair was in a tight bun, except for the few wild curls blowing in the breeze. Matthew could feel heat rise to his cheeks as she stood still before him.

Staring at each other for a long moment before running to each other's arms, he then held her and pressed her into him roughly. He bent his head to kiss her, but Mary Kate covered his mouth with her hand.

"Let's not be shameless!" she cried, though her eyes gave away how badly she really wanted his kiss.

"Mary Kate, if I don't kiss you soon, I will have to jump overboard to drown out the fire burning inside me!" Matthew's heart thumped loudly as his green eyes searched hers for a solution to this madness.

Grabbing her hand, Matthew led her down to the reception area near the chairs they sat in the first night they met. Thankfully, everyone was gone from the morning service. Pulling her into a secluded corner underneath the staircase by a tall palm plant, Matthew touched her face gently with his warm hands and locked his eyes with hers, breathing heavily at the thought of what was going to happen. They both knew that if they kissed, there was no turning back on their feelings.

All of Mary Kate's senses were alive, like little bubbles bursting one after another at this moment. The manly way Matthew smelled created a fire inside her body that she sought to quench. He had her in the corner, but it wasn't scary as when Ryan trapped her in the utility room.

Matthew nuzzled his face in her warm neck and kissed her eyes softly. Mary Kate could feel her willpower slipping away.

She grabbed the back of Matthew's head and planted his lips to hers. His lips were soft and warm, and she melted inside of his kiss. The couple kissed passionately for a few minutes, the kiss of passion that hadn't been unleashed in either of them until this moment. He was so relieved that she wanted him, too.

When their kiss finally broke apart, the couple gazed in each other's eyes for a long moment.

"Matthew, I don't know if I can tell you what I need to tell you." Mary Kate looked away from his passionate stare.

"Tell me, I will understand." Matthew bent down to kiss her again.

"No this is rather serious, it has to do with why I'm on this ship." Mary Kate pushed her way through Matthew, back out into the open area. If they were ever to be together, she had to tell him the truth now! He followed after her inquisitively. Mary Kate wrung her hands nervously and sighed.

"Can it be that bad? Are you a thief or, better yet, being sent out of Ireland for harlotry?"

"Please don't laugh, this is serious!"

Staring at her in disbelief, Matthew could sense her unwillingness to confess. "Well, I'm sorry. I didn't realize–"

"I'm going to be married to an American boy," Mary Kate blurted out.

Matthew gasped and stood with his mouth open for a minute.

"Matthew, I wanted to tell you sooner–"

"But you led me on! I thought you loved me!" Matthew spouted angrily, almost in mad tears.

Mary Kate took a step toward him, but he jerked away, repulsed. "Matthew, please! I do! Give me a chance to explain!" He stared at her as if she was a stranger, and it made her heart sink to her stomach. She had hurt him! He had to feel that this was not her intention!

Matthew asked icily, "So, is that who the picture is of?"

Mary Kate nodded, she realized then that he must have seen it when they accidentally switched books. If only he had said something to her that day!

"Matthew, I choose you. I don't want to marry William—" Mary Kate started.

"Please, spare me your explanation. I don't want to know his name or anything else. I just hope he makes you happy." Matthew could barely get through the sentence as tears clouded his green eyes. He turned around and walked off towards the elevator, dejected.

Mary Kate wanted to go after him, but she knew he wouldn't listen. A sad sigh escaped her as she returned to the stairs.

Neither Mary Kate nor Matthew knew that on the landing above stood Thomas. He had seen the whole act between the two lovers. He giggled and remarked to himself that this was perfect. This was going to be almost *too* easy.

Closing the door quietly to the stateroom, Matthew hoped Thomas wasn't around to make him feel worse. *How could it get any worse?* he thought. Matthew knew Mary Kate was going to America for something, and he always felt a lump form in his throat when he asked her about it. She was always hesitant to answer, and now he knew why. He flopped down on his bed and buried his face in his pillow and pounded on it with his fists.

Wasn't her kiss real though? When they danced? When he held her? Didn't she want him, too? He tortured himself with questions. His feelings for her had clouded his judgement. He hadn't meant to hurt her worse than she probably already was by telling him, but why couldn't she have told him sooner?

Matthew stood up and walked into the sitting area of the stateroom to pour himself a drink when the door burst open. Ryan and Thomas were standing there when Matthew looked up. He dropped the crystal glass to the floor, and the liquor splashed onto his brown shoes. Thomas slammed the door shut behind them, and he and Ryan came towards Matthew.

"No!" Matthew tried to wrestle free as Thomas held his arms behind his back.

"This is for you, loverboy!" Ryan taunted, and he put his hard fist into Matthew's stomach. Matthew made an awful retching noise and collapsed to the floor. Ryan had punched Matthew hard, and he shook out his fist, but yet it had felt so good to get some kind of revenge. Thomas picked his young master up off the floor and dropped him on the couch. Matthew held his stomach and writhed in pain.

"You are staying right here, while I go get your woman. Now I'm going to have her, pretty boy!" Ryan bent down in Matthew's face. Matthew grimaced, still in pain from Ryan's punch. Matthew groaned and tried to wrestle free as Thomas tied his hands together with the tie that went on the large drapes.

Matthew managed to say. "You won't get away with this—"

"Shut up!" Ryan slapped Matthew across his clean-shaven face. The stinging brought involuntary tears to his eyes and left a red handprint on his cheek. Thomas reached into Matthew's pocket and pulled out all the money he could find and handed a few crumpled bills to Ryan.

The conspirators locked the door and left Matthew in the stateroom.

"Now, you go see the girl." Ryan shook Thomas' sweaty hand as they sought to carry out their plan.

Knocking hesitantly on the same stateroom door she had just yesterday afternoon, Mary Kate sighed nervously, hoping no one saw her with all of Virginia's beautiful belonging in her hands. She would be more likely to be arrested than anything else.

The door opened, and a tall, good-looking young man stood

in front of her. His dark haircut, slightly longer on top, had been combed perfectly back, and his handsome demeanor made it unexplainably hard to withdraw her eyes.

"Hello there. I assume you are here to see Virginia." The young man smiled politely at her. Mary Kate just nodded, afraid to offend anyone with her unprivileged status. He motioned for her to come inside, and Mary Kate stepped hesitantly inside the familiar lavish stateroom and thanked the gentleman.

"Mary Kate!" Virginia came around the corner of the bedroom suite, then into the sitting area and opened her arms. Mary Kate smiled bleakly. She should not tell Virginia what happened this morning with Matthew.

"Oh, how rude of me. Mary Kate, this is David Worthington, my fiancé. And David, this is Matthew's friend, Mary Kate," Virginia introduced them.

"Very pleased to make your acquaintance." David extended his hand. Fumbling through the mass of clothes on her arm, Mary Kate took it.

"Same." Mary Kate smiled.

"Let me take those, dear. Do you have time to stay for tea?" Virginia turned and laid the clothes across the chair.

"No, really, I must go. But thank you for everything," Mary Kate answered quietly.

"Oh...." Virginia hesitated. "Is everything all right?" She could sense it wasn't.

Mary Kate nodded. "Yes, fine."

"Well, then, see you soon." Virginia smiled, her green eyes showing her concern.

"Yes, that would be great. Nice to meet you, Mr. Worthington." Mary Kate bowed her head in his direction and he did likewise as she turned and left Virginia's room for the last time.

Chapter 6

Mary Kate was on the poop deck, her arms resting on the rail. She wiped salty tears away from her eyes. Matthew had been so cold to her, but she deserved it! She should have told him the first day they met, not right after they had just shared their first kiss! Unfortunately, she did feel a sad sense of relief.

Mary Kate knew now that she had to go to America, to put Matthew and this whole trip behind her. She had to come through for her family and stay tied to her duty.

Bulky footsteps on the deck behind her were closing in on her, and she turned around, her heart racing. Maybe Matthew forgave her and was coming to tell her! Her heart dropped at the sight of a shabbily dressed obese man who she didn't recognize.

Mary Kate backed up against the rail, looking for a way to get past this man. "Who are you?"

"Well, actually, Miss, my master sent me." Then it dawned on Mary Kate that this must be Matthew's blithering butler!

"Really?" she said hopefully.

"Yes, Miss, he sent me this note for you." Thomas handed her a piece of White Star Line stationery, just like the one Matthew had written his cousin's stateroom number on.

"Can you read, Miss?" Thomas asked her, not knowing her abilities.

Mary Kate gave him a sour look and snatched the paper out of his hands. "Yes, I can read!" She unfolded the starchy white paper.

Etched in pencil, the note read:

Mary Kate,

I can't live without you. Please meet me tonight at ten o' clock at the grand stare case where we kissed today.
                                                    Matthew

Mary Kate noticed the word "staircase" was misspelled. She thought it odd that someone who was so avid a reader and so educated as Matthew would misspell such a simple word and have such awful handwriting. She looked at Thomas quizzically, then back at the paper. She and Matthew were the only ones that knew about their kiss this morning, though.

"How do I know this is really from Matthew?" Mary Kate asked suspiciously.

"Well, madam, Master Burnes said to bring this with you." Thomas opened his pudgy palm; there was the beautiful golden ring with the ruby Mary Kate had seen on Matthew's hand the day they met.

"He really wanted me to have this?" Mary Kate was more puzzled than ever as Thomas dropped the shiny ring in her quivering hand.

"Oh yes, Miss. As a token of his fondness and good intentions." Thomas bade her farewell and waddled off as slowly as he had come. Mary Kate watched Thomas walk away and looked at the note again. If Matthew wanted to talk, she would talk. She would listen to what he had to say, but she knew she must go to America now. Her brother and family were depending on her; she must not let a silly flirtation stand between her and her family.

Still groaning and writhing on the couch, Matthew managed to flop himself off the sofa and scoot over to the door. When he stood up, he could reach the doorknob but not get to the lock.

A knock came to the other stateroom door, in the adjoining room. Matthew grimaced as he tried to open the door that separated the two rooms so he could yell. The doorknob jiggled and came free! His stupid butler hadn't been smart enough to lock all the doors!

"I'm in here!" Matthew yelled desperately at the top of his lungs. Maybe it was Mary Kate and those bastards hadn't got to her yet. His heart leapt in his chest with anticipation.

"Matthew!" It was his cousin, Virginia. His cousin could help him get free, and then he could find Mary Kate before the two fiends got to her.

Virginia burst in through the unlocked door that went into the bedrooms of the stateroom. There was Matthew collapsed on the bed, his hands tied!

"Oh my God, Matthew!" Virginia threw her handbag on the bed and ran to her cousin. She frantically removed the small cord that bound her cousin's hands behind him.

"Oh, who did this to you?" Virginia cried frantically, feeling scared for her cousin.

"That's not important. I need to find Mary Kate right now." Matthew rubbed his raw wrists.

"How can you say that it isn't important?" Virginia grabbed her cousin by the shoulders. "Someone could have killed you!"

"Virginia, I can only tell you a few things that happened since last night. But you have to know that Mary Kate is who I love. I have to find her!" Matthew looked at his cousin with pleading eyes.

Virginia picked her black velvet clutch bag up from the bed and pulled it over her hand. "Matthew, do you realize what background she is from?"

"Of course, do you think I can't see that we're different?" Matthew shook his head.

"I just hope you realize that your father–"

"For once in my life, Virginia, I don't care what my father thinks!"

"I like Mary Kate very much. But she's not used to American life, Matthew."

"Are you trying to talk me out of doing what my heart tells me? Virginia, I know Mary Kate and I are of different worlds, but that is not going to stop me. I love her," Matthew somberly explained to his cousin.

"I know you do." The swish of Virginia's dress was the only sound as she went over to her cousin and put a reassuring arm around him.

"I can't describe the longing I feel for her when I look at her. Today she told me why she was going to America, and it doesn't even stop me from wanting her." Matthew seemed sad.

"Why is she going to America?" Virginia inquired.

"Well, she was going to marry an American boy." Virginia recoiled, shocked.

She took a step away from Matthew. "Oh my."

"Please don't be shocked, and please don't mention it if you see her. But if it's up to me, she's going to be my wife, not his. I don't think he gives a damn about her, and I don't even know the guy!" Matthew shook his finger angrily. He doubted in the back of his mind that Mary Kate would even talk to him after the way he had treated her.

Virginia smiled at her cousin. Years ago they were so young and simple. Status didn't matter. Now, within the short space of a couple of weeks, they had both found love.

"Matthew...." Virginia began, "we'd better not let her get away then."

Chapter 7

Mary Kate looked at Patrick's gold timepiece. The one he had received from her father when he turned eighteen. Mary Kate swallowed the lump of guilt in her throat at the image of her father's face in her mind. It was ten until ten. Getting up from the bottom bunk slowly, she walked towards the door. She knew Patrick wouldn't hear her go out, he had been drinking and smoking too heavily the last few days and was catching up on his rest. Mary Kate closed the door quietly behind her, she had to find Matthew and tell him good-bye. She had to fulfill her duty to her family.

Unable to eat supper, Mary Kate couldn't read her book or do much else after what happened with Matthew. Then his mysterious letter and request to meet him tonight.

Mary Kate made her way quickly to the 'D' deck, a way that she knew for certain now after following Matthew around. The ship seemed very dark to her, but it was nearly ten o'clock on Sunday night, and the lights were turned off to encourage people to retire to their rooms.

Mary Kate stood in the dark reception area before the first-class dining saloon. She noticed the corner where her and Matthew kissed. Heat rose to her cheeks, and she looked away quickly. Her leather boots clicking on the marble floor was the only sound. She heard a noise in the corner.

"Matthew?" She turned around abruptly towards the noise, her heart pounding fiercely. Footsteps came closer to her, and then light reflected off his face. It was Ryan! She knew deep down right from the beginning that something was wrong with this whole situation!

Mary Kate cried out as Ryan put his sweaty hand over her mouth and backed her into the same corner where she and Matthew first kissed.

In his excitement, Ryan knocked over the palm plant, spilling dirt all over the floor. Thomas came up behind Ryan and kept looking over his shoulder to watch for staff or passersby.

Pinning her in the corner with his elbow, Ryan shoved his knee up in her stomach. The hand he still held over her mouth muffled Mary Kate's cry.

Mary Kate was overcome with fear and panic. There was no one to help her! Matthew was still mad at her, and he never wrote that letter or wanted to see her, it was a farce created by Ryan! The hope she had earlier that Matthew still wanted her was dashed. She had no reason to even be here, and Patrick would sleep right through it, because he was several decks below!

Mary Kate tried to cry out, but her mouth was covered. She couldn't let this happen! She lifted her leg and stepped down as hard as she could on Ryan's foot with her leather boot heel.

"God damn it!" Ryan cried out, and he loosened his elbow enough for Mary Kate to scramble free. Ryan grabbed her leg, and she toppled to the floor, facedown, screaming for help.

"Jesus, man, make her be quiet!" Ryan yelled at Thomas, but Thomas was too slow and fat to stoop down to the floor to cover her mouth. Ryan grabbed Mary Kate's shoulders and pulled her into an upright standing position. He locked his fierce eyes with her fearful blue ones. It excited him that she looked as afraid as an animal caught in a trap.

"Ya're gonna pay for that!" Ryan slapped her white cheek, leaving a red handprint, as several pairs of footsteps came charging into the reception hall.

Matthew! And Patrick, too! Flanked by two White Star Line staff. Virginia was there, too, with David. They had all come to save her, and Mary Kate began to sob with relief.

Patrick grabbed Ryan as the guards caught up with Thomas. Matthew's first concern was Mary Kate, and he grabbed her and held her tightly.

"Oh my God, I would have come sooner, but they tied me up and...." Matthew whispered in her ear, as she hung on to his strong frame with all her might.

"I'm sorry, I don't mean to cry!" Mary Kate sobbed. Matthew hushed her and held her closer than ever to him. He rocked back and forth gently with her and patted her auburn locks. He recalled thinking of how pretty he thought she was the day he met her.

Patrick helped the White Star Line guards haul off the two men to the master-at-arms office below deck. As he looked at his sister and her lover, Patrick was sure now that he was powerless to stop their love. Virginia and David smiled at each other and decided to leave the couple in silence.

Matthew held Mary Kate close for a long time. Mary Kate didn't ever want to let go, and she knew now that she wanted Matthew, not William, no matter what the consequences.

"Matthew, there is something I need to tell you." Mary Kate stopped sniffling and looked into his warm eyes.

"Oh, not again!" Matthew smiled his bright white smile at her, referring to this morning's confession.

"No, it's not like that. The day after I met you, Ryan trapped me in a utility room. He said you were with some other girl.... I didn't believe him. But I had a fear he has been trying to get to me since, I never knew...." Mary Kate confessed.

"Why didn't you tell me?" Matthew grabbed her small chin with his hand and brought her eyes to meet his.

Mary Kate just shrugged and looked up at him with wide, apologetic eyes.

"You know that isn't true anyway, don't you? The only woman I look at is you, and my cousin if you can count her!" Matthew teased her.

They stayed silent for a while longer, Matthew rested his chin on top of her head and tried to find the courage to tell her what he wanted to say.

"Mary Kate, I've decided I'm not leaving this ship without you. Don't say anything, but we will find that boy you're supposed to marry. If you decide that you want him instead of me, I understand, but all I ask is that you just let me be with you until then."

"You know, I used to feel sick to my stomach every time I looked at the picture of William. My Aunt Opal arranged this whole marriage, and I used to feel so guilty about ever having to tell you, but why should I feel guilty about breaking the heart of a man I never met?" Mary Kate smiled warmly, at peace with her decision.

"You broke my heart earlier, but I forgive you," Matthew said to her softly, and he kissed her white forehead.

"So, how did you ever meet up with Patrick?" Mary Kate looked curiously at Matthew.

"Well … Thomas and Ryan came to my room and beat me up and tied my hands behind my back–"

"Oh, Matthew!"

"It could have been worse, I was just worried for you."

"So how did you get free?"

Their embrace broke apart as Matthew relayed his story, "There are two doors to the stateroom, one in the bedroom, and one in the sitting area, I was bound in the sitting area. Virginia knocked on the other door, so I managed to holler loud enough for her to come and untie my hands. Lucky for me she came by, or else who knows? Then we set about finding you. I looked everywhere, and finally I got up enough nerve to go see your brother. He said he hadn't heard you go out, and I knew that you were in trouble, I just knew. So Patrick and I looked together and asked some crew members, they thought they had seen a girl of your description, so we came as fast as we could. For some reason, I knew you must be here. This seems to be our favorite spot on the ship!" Matthew told her, referring to the room they were standing in.

"Matthew, do you believe things happen for a reason? Like in a Dickens novel?"

"What?" Matthew chuckled.

"Do you believe that we were meant to be here, on this ship, to meet each other?"

"Yes, I do. Mary Kate, I was sure before the day I met you that I would never love anybody. Then you were just sent to me, right before my eyes! I still can't believe it."

"Yes, I did run into you actually."

"Yes, you actually did! If it weren't for our love of books, we might not have ever talked again!" Matthew laughed, and Mary Kate put her hand over his mouth.

"Don't say that! We are together now. That's all that matters." Matthew smiled at her warmly.

"Do you know, that someday, I'm going to take you on this ship again. We might be old and gray, but I'm going to work hard for us, Mary Kate. You'll see. Then we can relive this April that we met each other." Matthew lifted her heart-shaped face to his and kissed her softly on the lips.

"Matthew, I really don't deserve this. I could have been destined to spend the rest of my life being a strange man's slave. You saved me!" Mary Kate snuggled into Matthew's warm shoulder, and he patted her hair softly.

The couple stayed quiet for a few minutes, just long enough to hear the steady humming of the engines change and feel a variance in the vibration.

"Did you hear that? It sounds different," Matthew mentioned, still holding on tightly to Mary Kate.

"No, I really can't tell, but it feels different, I suppose." Clasping hands, they walked over to the large windows on either side of the reception room, on the starboard side of the ship.

Before either one could say anything else, their view was blocked by an eerie white and blue sheet, and they felt a slight bump underneath them.

"What the devil was that?" Mary Kate cried anxiously.

Matthew turned to her with fear in his eyes.

"I think it was an iceberg!"

Chapter 8

Lights came back on all over the ship. Tension was in the air as word was passed along that *Titanic* had struck an iceberg.

Mary Kate followed Matthew up to the boat deck. A few lingering chunks of ice could still be seen on the lower decks. Some men were in their pajamas picking the ice chunks up and joking about putting it in their drinks.

"It's cold out here!" Mary Kate folded her arms across her chest. As she exhaled, her warm breath streamed into the night air.

"I know, we can go back inside, I just wanted to see what all the fuss was about." Matthew leaned over the rail, looking back at the iceberg.

"What ya think, mate, gotta be over a hundred feet tall?" A passing pair of crewmembers were talking to each other as they passed Mary Kate and Matthew. Mary Kate looked at Matthew and then to the door. It was rather cold, and she wanted to go inside. Matthew stepped off the rail and came over to Mary Kate.

"We'd better go," he said, panicked. Mary Kate was startled, but she followed Matthew anyway.

Compared to the noise outside on the boat deck and at the grand staircase, Matthew's stateroom was very quiet.

Matthew was busily stuffing things in his pockets while Mary Kate combed her hair and rearranged it back into a bun.

"As soon as we can, we are going to get to a lifeboat." Matthew stated.

Mary Kate turned to him with wide blue eyes.

"Didn't you ever notice the amount of lifeboats? There aren't enough for everyone, so we'd better get to one quickly."

Matthew took Mary Kate's arm. Her gaze became clouded, and she looked at Matthew fearfully.

"What? What is it?" Matthew grabbed her by the shoulders.

"My brother, Patrick, what will become of him?" Mary Kate asked with a quivering voice.

Matthew just looked at her for a few seconds, then turned away, not answering her.

Mary Kate groaned, "No, no!"

"It's true, first-class passengers will board lifeboats first. This may be the only time being rich will save me."

"But this ship isn't going to really sink, is it? It's supposed to be unsinkable!" Mary Kate cried, clinging to false hope.

"There is nothing in this world that can not be taken down by the hand of God!" Matthew cried, continuing to frantically go through his belongings. Mary Kate was beginning to see a side of Matthew that scared her.

"I'm going back to my brother," she said sternly. Matthew whipped around and shook his head fervently.

"No, you can't! I've waited all my life to find you and I've been through hell for you today; please don't do this!" Matthew pleaded.

"Please, Matthew, he is my family and he needs me! I could never forgive myself if he perished and I lived to fulfill my selfishness!"

"Mary Kate, think about what you just said. If you go back, you won't come back up. You will go to the bottom of the ocean with everyone else down there!" Matthew's hysterics were beginning to frighten her.

Mary Kate looked away from his gaze. Her heart was breaking, she could feel it splinter into a thousand pieces.

"Matthew, I have to go, I'm sorry." Mary Kate left the room

quietly. Matthew, shocked, watched her go. After she left, his heart sank to the bottom of his stomach. He would finish rounding up some valuables and then find her.

"Where is that god damn ring?" Matthew bellowed.

Running as fast as she could, Mary Kate hurried past the palm court where she and Matthew danced outside, past the grand staircase where her and Matthew first kissed, past the red velvet chairs where they sat and talked the first night they met. That all seemed so far away now, like it was so long ago. Terror struck Mary Kate's heart. If she had just been a good girl, then none of this ever would have happened!

Mary Kate ran down the stairs leading to the lower decks, against a steadily increasing flow of traffic. People began to fear the worst, and those who could were streaming up to the boat deck. She approached the landing of the deck where she would descend to go to her cabin, but a black iron gate blocked her way.

"No, no!" Mary Kate rattled the gate frantically when she heard terrified cries coming from further down the passageway. She walked hesitantly around the corner to see a White Star Line steward standing in front of the same type of gate that had separated her from the lower decks. He was trying to calm the people wanting to ascend to the upper decks.

Mary Kate inched further toward the gate, seeing the fear in the people's eyes. No one believed that the ship would sink, it couldn't sink. She heard someone's horrid cry that his or her cabin was taking on water. She heard another person's rage at the steward for not opening the gate. There were cries in strange languages that she did not recognize. But the look of terror on their faces did not need language.

"Mary Kate!" she heard her brother's familiar gruff voice.

"Patrick!" Mary Kate rushed to the gate, and the steward tried to pull her away.

"No, God damn you! That's my sister! Let me talk to her!" Patrick cried, and the steward backed away.

Locking hands through the spaces in the black wrought-iron gate, the sibling's hands were clasped so tight that their knuckles had turned white.

"Mary Kate, listen to me, you have to get up to the boat deck right away, the water is gettin' higher down here!" Patrick pleaded with his sister.

"No, Patrick!" Mary Kate shook her head.

"Yes, you have to!" Sean pleaded, too. Looking from her brother to Sean, Mary Kate wondered if Sean knew what his brother Ryan had tried to do this evening.

"No, I can't. I came back for you!" Mary Kate shivered, not from the cold water seeping in the ship, but from the adrenaline coursing through her veins.

Patrick sighed impatiently. "I thought you were with Matthew, where is he?"

"I left him to come to you. He didn't want me to, but I can't do this!"

"Mary Kate, you have to go back up!"

"No! I won't!"

"You must go now!" Patrick pointed his rugged finger up the stairwell, and his brown eyes blazed with fury.

"This ship isn't going to sink, is it?" Mary Kate still couldn't believe it. Patrick and Sean looked at each other with a knowing look.

"You know, they aren't going to open this gate, girl!" Sean cried, affirming Patrick.

"GO!" Patrick urged her again.

Mary Kate looked around, people behind the gate were afraid; she could see the fear in their eyes. *Oh my God.* They knew they were going to die.

Mary Kate hesitated a few minutes, then kissed Patrick on his rough, bearded face through a space in the gate. She nodded good-bye to Sean. She and Patrick locked sad eyes; eyes wide open as if to soak up in their memories the last time they would ever see each other.

Salty tears ran down Mary Kate's rosy cheeks as she let go of her brother's rough hand. She ascended to the next deck level without looking back. She couldn't bear to see the look of death in her brother's eyes as she had in those others.

Chapter 9

Sitting silently on the couch in the sitting area of his stateroom, Matthew scratched the five o'clock shadow beginning to grow on his square chin. He was sad beyond description, but he didn't really know what to do. He had gone to the boat deck to wait for a lifeboat, but the crew was only loading women and children right now. He was glad he was in privacy in his own room, because people were now beginning to crowd the areas near the boat deck.

Silently, he cursed himself. Why had he let her leave? He should have physically held Mary Kate there with him. Why didn't he go get her? Demand she come with him? She went below decks, and he was sure he might not find her again. Why did she leave? he demanded of himself. She took his love, then flew away like a thief in the night.

Virginia knocked quietly on the door.

"Enter," Matthew said from the couch, and he took a big swig from one of Thomas' new bottles of brandy.

"Oh, Matthew!" Virginia and David entered his room. Virginia bustled over to the couch and knelt down by her cousin.

Matthew said, no emotion in his voice, "Please don't worry for me. You two'd better go to a lifeboat soon. I think I can feel the ship listing."

"Please come up on deck with us. Put a life-belt on and come up there with us." Virginia's green eyes were wet with tears.

"No, I don't want to do this anymore. I don't know if she wants me to chase her down again, but I'm just so tired!" Matthew began to cry, and he was ashamed to break down in front of his cousin and her fiancé, but he couldn't help it. Mary Kate leaving to go back to her brother was the last straw. Virginia put a comforting arm around Matthew, and she looked at David helplessly. David smiled heart-brokenly at his fiancée.

"Please try for our sake, we love you." Virginia held Matthew's shoulders as they shook with sobs.

"No." Matthew looked up at his cousin, his eyes red. "You go get your life-belt on and get up there. I would rather just stay here. Go on! Leave me be," Matthew begged. Virginia stood up and went to David as he wrapped a reassuring arm around her thin waist.

"I can't bear to know I left you behind," Virginia said before leading David to the door.

"It's my fault, all my fault." Matthew looked at her and motioned for her to leave. Virginia and David looked at each other sadly before closing the door.

Matthew sighed and pulled his handkerchief out of his coat pocket. He blew his nose with a loud honk and looked out his window. The ocean was definitely getting closer to his window.

Mary Kate sat stonily on a deck chair on the boat deck by the crew's bridge. Her head hurt from crying, and she lifted her eyes as a distress flare shot from the sky on the other side of the bridge from her. Sounds of fear and anticipation rang in her ears.

"Women and children only at this time!"

The seaman waved people towards him as he helped them in the large lifeboat. The clunk of footsteps on the wooden boat deck, heading towards lifeboats. The unhappy cries of women and children being separated from their husbands and fathers. She could hear the music the band played in vain to try and keep the passengers calm. Some went with hope in their hearts that they would meet again. Others refused to be separated. Mary Kate's heart felt low when she thought of herself being separated from her brother. The beginning of the end was happening in front of her. She shivered and wrapped her arms around herself tighter. The shawl she had been wearing all day was not much warmth now.

Mary Kate sighed, and suddenly a black-and-white plaid blanket was thrust in her face. She looked up and saw a young crewman who had noticed her chill standing in front of her, holding the blanket.

"This will keep you warm, love," he said sweetly.

"Thank you for your kindness." Mary Kate thanked him and graciously let him wrap the warm blanket around her chilled soul.

"Can I help you to a boat, Miss?" he asked quietly.

Mary Kate shook her head sadly and held up her hand. "No, thank you."

"Miss, are you sure?"

"Yes, and I'm sorry, but my brother is below deck in third class. It seems unlikely that he will get to a boat, and I could not forgive myself if I left him here to die." Mary Kate looked down at her hands. The crewman nodded his head in agreement and extended his large white hand.

"There's so much else to live for though, isn't there?" Mary Kate looked at his outstretched hand, then up to his warm brown eyes.

"I suppose, but not for me."

"My name is Fifth Officer Harold Lowe. Please come with me to a boat," the young man pleaded, and Mary Kate remained silent. She looked into the young man's face. Why should he care so much about whether she lived or not? Mary Kate's heart sank again when she thought of her brother, who wanted her to live, but she could not leave him behind!

"I'm sorry." Mary Kate turned away from the young man's gaze with tears forming in her eyes. Refusing to give up, the young officer returned a few minutes later with a white life-belt. It was designed to fit over the head like an apron, with ties on the sides and separately sewn-in rectangular flotation pieces, six in front and six in back.

"Please put this on, Miss. Do it for me?" Mary Kate smiled weakly, she admired his perseverance, and took the life-belt. Officer Lowe helped her get it over her head and tie it.

"If you change your mind about a lifeboat, please tell me. But a warning to you that they are filling up fast." He smiled at her, tipped his hat, and headed aft towards the stern of the ship.

Chapter 10

Mary Kate looked down at her cold hands, and she still shivered from the cold air. She wondered what Matthew was doing, probably already on one of the many lifeboats that rowed away from the large ship.

Everyone was waiting for the ship to sink. At first, the passengers were told that the loading of lifeboats was precautionary. Now everyone knew the real demise they were in.

Mary Kate pulled her bun apart; hoping her hair would help keep her warm. Her elbow-length auburn curls spilled across her shoulders. She wrapped the blanket tighter around her. She could hear water spilling across the front of the ship as the weight of the water forced it to creak and groan. The darkness scared her. When the ship went down, she would have nothing to cling to, because there were no rocks as near shore. The lifeboats were so scattered that it would be hard to find one. The water was so cold that it would make it hard to swim to a lifeboat even if you could find one.

Shivering again, Mary Kate thought of how cold the water must be. She reached up and touched her nose; it was red from the cold air that tingled her face. The stars above her twinkled happily, oblivious to what went on below them. Then Matthew's words occurred to her, about nothing being above God's hand. It made sense to her now. Was God doing this to prove man was nothing but a simple animal that could not outsmart His power? Was this God's will to prove to the world that man could build bigger and faster machines but still not overpower His might?

Looking up at the stars again, Mary Kate noticed how they scattered across the night sky like sparkles, and it did not comfort her to know that her father might be looking at the same stars back home.

Footsteps came up behind her and stopped abruptly, and she looked up into Matthew's face!

"Matthew!" Mary Kate cried and stood up, the blanket toppling from her shoulders.

Another distress flare shot white flames into the night sky as they embraced for several moments before either one spoke.

"Did you find your brother?" Matthew asked her, wrapping one of her cold curls around his finger.

"Yes, I did. But there was a gate … it blocked.…" Beginning to cry, Mary Kate leaned into Matthew's strong shoulder once again. Matthew hushed her and held her close.

"Don't cry, there's nothing you can do."

"He begged me to get on a lifeboat, but I just can't live knowing he's down there! He said the water was coming up down there and they are trapped!" Mary Kate sobbed.

"Oh, that's awful." Matthew sympathized, yet he knew he was powerless to help, too.

"Matthew, it's awful, they are caged down there like animals! They won't let them up to the boat deck!" Mary Kate sobbed tears for all the people that were trapped in the belly of the ship. Matthew comforted her as best he could and quietly held her.

The slant of the ship toward the bow was becoming evident to those standing on her decks, and the urge to press toward the stern came upon many people.

"I came to find you to get you on a boat." Matthew lifted her chin to look in her eyes.

"I don't want to. Everyone else is going to die, why can't I?

94

Then I won't be alone."

"Don't talk like that!"

"But it's true."

"You have to go, Mary Kate. I won't have you talk like that."

"Only if you go with me."

"They are only putting on women and children right now, but I can meet up with you later."

"Matthew! Don't you understand!" Mary Kate thumped on his chest angrily with her fist.

"Stop it!"

"You said so yourself there are not enough boats!"

"I can swim, don't worry about me."

"Matthew, that water has to be as cold as the air, or colder, you wouldn't be able to swim for long!" Mary Kate began to cry again.

Looking at her helplessly, Matthew knew she was right. If he lived long enough not to drown, he would surely freeze to death in the icy cold waters of the North Atlantic Ocean.

Another white flare shot into the night sky. People continued heading toward the lifeboats when Matthew heard the water splashing up near the front of the ship. Urgently, he grabbed Mary Kate's arm and pulled her up the deck.

"We can't stay here for long, there can't be much time left." Matthew whipped her around to face him. He thought sadly that it might be the last time he looked in her beautiful eyes. Mary Kate stared at Matthew, hoping he could come up with a swift plan to save them both. She had had to say good-bye to Patrick; she didn't want to have to tell Matthew farewell either.

"What should we do?" Mary Kate asked Matthew, hanging on to his strong arm.

"You have to go to a boat. There are not many left, and now don't give me that look," Matthew scolded her for pouting at him.

"But I can't survive on my own. What shall I do until I find you?"

"There is nothing you can do but just wait in the lifeboat. The crew will tell you what to do."

"Matthew, I want you more than anything, I can't go without you."

"You must, I won't hear any more." He grabbed her arm again and pulled her up the deck to one of the few remaining boats on the port side of *Titanic*.

Matthew grabbed her face and stared into her eyes sincerely. "Mary Kate, I want you to know that I am going to find you. Don't give up hope. I will not rest until I find you, and I will not forget. I promise." Matthew leaned forward and kissed her softly on the lips. His whiskers poked her soft skin, but it was nice to be close to Matthew.

Smiling, Mary Kate squeezed Matthew's soft warm hand, and she hoped to God things would be all right. Matthew didn't seem very worried, but he was a much smarter traveler. Mary Kate trusted him and knew if there was reason to be worried, he would tell her.

The couple waited for a lifeboat behind some other people. Another flare was jetted into the black velvet night. Mary Kate and Matthew inched closer to the boat, which was almost full. The ropes made a searing noise as they slipped through the davits.

"Next woman or child, please!" Mary Kate recognized the voice of Officer Lowe. She stepped forward, and he smiled at her. He grabbed her hand and helped her step into the lifeboat. It felt strange to have the boat swing as she was stepping into it. One of the ladies in the boat reached her hand out to help Mary Kate steady herself. Taking her seat on the outside seat still nearest the ship, Mary Kate and Matthew smiled nervously at each other.

"Take her down!" The boat began to lower with a sharp jolt.

Several women on board gasped, and Mary Kate put her hands out to steady herself. She looked back at Matthew with a fearful look. He smiled at her, his bright teeth showing. She smiled to herself when she noticed his disheveled look. The first day she met him, she thought him so handsome and clean. Now he looked so funny with his whiskers growing wild, his hair tousled, and his shirt collar undone. She stretched the yarn of her shawl as she fought to keep warm underneath her.

"Good-bye," he mouthed to her silently, and Mary Kate continued to look into his face. She wished she was dreaming, and she would wake up soon.

At the next deck level, people tried to swarm the boat.

"Stay back!" Officer Lowe screamed. He fired three shots in the air with his revolver, and Mary Kate shuddered with fear. She covered her ears with her hands to drown out the mounting anxiety. When she looked back up, Matthew's face had disappeared from sight.

"Don't you have a coat, dear?" an elegant lady sitting next to Mary Kate asked her, and she wrapped her arms around the shivering girl. Shaking her head, Mary Kate strained to see the lady in the dark. Mary Kate turned to face the black iron that the lifeboat swung so close to. The black iron that was supposed to keep her passengers safe but had given way to an iceberg. Mary Kate shivered again. Matthew had said there was nothing in this world that couldn't be taken down by God, and now it was being proven.

The boat lowered slowly, and Mary Kate could do nothing but stare at the blackness of the ship until the boat slowly entered the dark ocean and was cut away. It began to row away steadily from *Titanic,* like a stray kitten from its mother.

Watching from the deck, Matthew saw the ship row away, and he swallowed the lump in his throat. He didn't want to lie to Mary Kate, but he had to make sure she was safe. He walked silently back to the grand staircase where some people were still congregated. He no more than entered his stateroom, when water began to filter into the reception area before the first-class dining saloon.

Chapter 11

Sitting back silently in a boat, Mary Kate watched the lighted ship tip facedown in the icy waters. She could hear the horrified screams of people who were making their way as fast as they could to the stern of the ship. In the darkness, she could barely see them, and from so far away they looked so small. It didn't seem possible to Mary Kate that it was the same ship she left her brother behind on, the same ship Matthew had come to her on. She kept wishing it were a dream, a horrible dream. It was as if she was watching it all happen from a mile away.

She could hear the terrible groaning of the ship as it gave way to the powerful ocean. There was a horrible snapping and whining noise as the first funnel crumpled into the ocean. Several ladies on the lifeboat cried helplessly. *Titanic*'s doom was apparent now, and reality set in on Mary Kate, too. She thought of Patrick's face the last time she saw him. The last touch of her kiss on his rough face. She thought of Matthew's face as she lowered away in the lifeboat, she could still see his gray-green eyes piercing her soul. She had to sense in her heart that they were going to die! There was no way around it, if they got out to the deck, they would die in the cold ocean. Hanging her head, Mary Kate cried silently, and the woman next to her heard her and pulled her closer into her shoulder. But Mary Kate could find no comfort.

Everyone watched the once-magnificent ship, still lit up, giving way to the ocean. All felt helpless, when would there be another ship to come rescue them?

Mary Kate stared in dismay as the ship appeared to stand vertical. The ropes that had swung out the lifeboats hung limply against her black iron girth. Her lights flickered, then everything went dark. No one moved for several minutes, and no one realized how much light the ship had given. Now everything was dark, only a ghostly outline of the massive ship stood out against the dark sky. There was nothing to see, but she could hear the fearsome cries of people still on the looming ship. Its massive propellers could be seen. Working only a short while ago, they were still.

A terrifying snapping and creaking noise filled the air as the back end of the ship separated itself from the front half. A thousand screams pierced the black night as the stern fell back on the ocean with a massive splash and a thunderous roar. The fourth funnel tore from the ship and clanked noisily onto the deck of the ship, then rolled into the ocean.

The only sound now was the bone-chilling gurgling and chugging noises of the massive ship as it hurtled to the bottom of the Atlantic Ocean. The people in lifeboats could only watch her descent with gaping jaws and wide eyes.

Mary Kate covered her ears to silence thousands of horrid cries that echoed across the black ocean. Nothing she could do could drown them out. She shivered helplessly. One of those cries might be Matthew. Another one might be Patrick.

There was barely a splash where the modern wonder once stood, only people in their life-belts. Freezing and crying. Splashing helplessly, wanting the lifeboats to come back. Waiting.

"Maybe another ship is coming to save them!" another lady in their lifeboat cried hopefully.

The screams and cries continued, echoing through Mary Kate's ears like a thousand drums. She remembered the happy choruses and cheers and whistles as the ship left Southampton not even a week ago. Now they were horrid cries of a dream that was supposed to end happily. She covered her ears again and prayed.

"Hail Mary, full of grace, the Lord is with thee, blessed art thou amongst women and blessed is the fruit of thy womb Jesus. Holy Mary, Mother of God, pray for us sinners now and at the hour of our death, Amen," she repeated over and over to herself.

The cries finally ended after half an hour or so, but no one was happy to hear it stop. They knew what it meant when the din ceased.

Now the only sounds were crying from the lifeboats and the gentle lapping of the ocean against the sides of the lifeboats. This wasn't supposed to happen. Everyone was shocked into silence. How could this happen to the grandest ship in the world? Could this be real?

The ocean was so dark. The only lights were the stars that dotted the inky blackness and reflected off the still ocean. There was no moon, nothing but blackness. Mary Kate felt so small. Everywhere around her, all she could feel was blackness, and she never realized how vast the ocean was. It was vast enough to open up and swallow the biggest ship ever. Every once in a while she thought she could see the outline of something against the sky. She wondered if they were icebergs, laughing at the passengers and people of *Titanic*, who had thrown caution to the wind and lost. There was a far-off light in the distance, and many on Mary Kate's lifeboat wondered if it belonged to another ship. But the light never moved closer, it remained still.

Officer Lowe pulled up alongside another lifeboat and had them tied together. He urged everyone in his boat to go into the other lifeboats, and he smirked at Mary Kate as he helped her weak body move into the new lifeboat. Everyone followed his orders, and Officer Lowe, along with a few other crewmen, rowed off to find any survivors. He went even though others warned him those struggling to survive might swamp his boat. But brave Officer Lowe in his heart knew he might not find anyone alive.

Convulsing with cold shivers, Mary Kate still prayed this were a dream. People on the lifeboats huddled together to keep warm, wondering what would become of them. Would they float forever? Mary Kate had no sensation left in her feet. Everything was happening so fast that she wasn't concerned with anything other than the pain in her body or her heart.

A lady next to her wrapped her warm arms around the young girl and pulled her close, patting her hair. A woman who, if the ship had stayed afloat, probably wouldn't have even looked at her twice because of their differences in status.

Silently, Mary Kate wondered if Matthew and Patrick would be all right. She also wondered about Matthew's cousin, Virginia, and her fiancé. What would happen to all those people she met? As the lifeboat floated freely, Mary Kate's mind wandered back and forth over many subjects.

Mary Kate had time to wonder about many things. She thought about when she first learned she was going to America, and on *Titanic*. She thought about her brother's sweet face and how he gruffly loved her in his own way. She thought about Matthew, and how if it weren't for him, she might never have been so happy. She missed him terribly already and knew deep in her heart she may never see him again. She tried to tell herself it was all right and she wouldn't miss him, because he would live. He had to live; it just wasn't fair if he didn't.

Mary Kate's stomach twisted in a knot when she remembered her first day on the ship. The weird little Englishman and his premonition of disaster. How did he know? Why didn't she listen? Oh my God, his horrible prediction was true! Mary Kate was too cold to cry, but she wondered if indeed the stranger had disembarked the ship as he said he would. Maybe it was her sign from God, and she had chosen to ignore it! Dear God, had her sin caused everyone's misfortune? She couldn't help but feel partially to blame for what had happened. Maybe if she just would have stayed below deck and fulfilled her promise of going to America. Instead she fell in love with someone she never would have met if it weren't for William or her Aunt Opal!

Mary Kate's head throbbed. There was too much to think about and remember from this whole trip. America was not turning out to be nearly as great as she thought before she left Ireland. Dear God, how would her father feel when he found out about Patrick's plight? How would her father feel when he found out Mary Kate's sin had caused it all? Mary Kate shook her head solemnly. She was still shivering convulsively, and it was too cold to cry.

Chapter 12

Mary Kate went in and out of sleep. Sometimes her head would bow, and she would doze for a few minutes. She would nearly snap her neck when she remembered where she was and why, and she would unwillingly come back into consciousness. She would be in disbelief for a minute and almost start to cry, however, her exhaustion would eventually outweigh her sadness, and her head would bow, and she would repeat the cycle again.

Paying no attention to the mumblings coming from the other boats, Mary Kate didn't want to hear the silent pleas and prayers that were in vain. She had to realize there was no hope for those who had been spilled into the ocean when *Titanic* sank. It was so cold that she nearly was frozen, without ever having touched the water.

"A ship!" Mary Kate heard someone cry. She opened her eyes slowly and saw a green light shining out against the darkness. Everything was still so black that only the outline of a ship could be seen, and she could faintly hear voices coming from it. Green rockets fired from the ship as it treaded slowly toward them. Their lifeboat began to row steadily toward the ship, and Mary Kate felt a sad sense of relief.

The dawn began to appear over the dark horizon, and slowly it became light. Mary Kate could see the ice that sent *Titanic* to her fate. The ice reflected blue and violet; like a rainbow of colors before her weary eyes. How ironic that such beauty at daybreak had brought about such terror in the night.

Young William Richter sat at the shiny mahogany table that Monday morning, his black coffee quivering in his hand.

"Anything the matter, sir?" the maid asked quietly, watching the look on her young master's face turn to horror.

"Go fetch Mrs. Opal Hamling. Fast as you can!" William ordered sharply, his brown eyes ablaze. The young maid curtsied and abided the rules. William set the paper down on the long table and read the headline again to be sure he read it correctly. ***TITANIC** SINKS – LARGE LOSS OF LIFE.*

An eternity passed before the lifeboat pulled alongside the ship. She could read the name; *Carpathia*. Mary Kate had little feeling in her feet, and a crewman helped her aboard. She was first taken into the ship's dining saloon to receive medical attention and given a warm blanket and some hot water. Mary Kate then thankfully let another steward lead her down to the stern of the Cunard ship, and he sat her down and handed her another blanket. Mary Kate undid her leather boots and removed her frozen stockings. Two toes on her left foot looked purple, but she thought nothing of it and moved them into the sunshine to gather heat. It was eerily quiet on the rescue ship. Either no one could believe what happened, or they didn't want to talk about it.

A crewman returned with a cup of coffee, which Mary Kate gladly accepted. As he turned to leave, Mary Kate grabbed his hand. The young man looked at her sorrowfully.

He asked, "Can I help you, Miss?"

"Yes, do you have any word on survivors yet?" she gasped.

"I can find out for you, although not all lifeboats have boarded yet."

"Please let me know when they have, I am looking for two people."

"Yes, Miss." The young man left her with horror and pity on his face.

"Mary Kate!" a man's voice cried hoarsely, Mary Kate's heart leapt with joy when she turned around.

Mary Kate turned around; she did not recognize the man. He looked vaguely familiar, but she couldn't think of his name.

"Mary Kate!" The young man stepped closer.

Mary Kate asked, afraid, "Yes?"

"It's David, Virginia's fiancé." Then instantly Mary Kate recognized him. He looked very rough compared to when she met him first. He sat down next to Mary Kate and pulled the dark blanket around him.

"Oh, Dear God!" Mary Kate fell into his lap and put her arms around him. She had met him only once but felt so relieved. Surely, Matthew and his cousin would be with David!

Mary Kate sat back and took his hand. Tears were in both their eyes.

"Please tell me Matthew and Virginia are with you, tell me please!" Mary Kate pleaded.

"Oh, how I wish I could." David rubbed his eyes as if to stop the tears coming from it.

"Oh no, oh no!" Mary Kate shook her head.

"I tried to get Virginia to a boat, but she refused! We floated for...." David cried out.

"You tried, please, you tried!"

"But I should have insisted."

"It's too late now, please...." Mary Kate trailed off. She reached behind her and grabbed the coffee that was rapidly cooling off in the cold air. David took it thankfully and calmed down slowly.

"We tried to get Matthew on a boat, too. He was too distraught to go." David looked at Mary Kate curiously, expecting her to say something.

"He met up with me again. He put me on a lifeboat, and I did not see him after that," Mary Kate said sadly.

David said nothing, but they both had the same thought;

Matthew would have needed a miracle to have lived. *Patrick would have needed a bigger miracle than Matthew to live*, Mary Kate sadly thought

"I think there is a prayer service in the dining saloon tonight? Would you join with me?" David asked her as he finished the coffee.

"Of course I will. I think we need God more than anything right now." Mary Kate smiled as best she could at him and took his hand.

Snuggling close to David, Mary Kate noticed people of every race and class began to congregate in the large dining saloon of the *Carpathia*. Captain Rostron approached the front with his slight frame and removed his hat. He sighed, as everyone there knew what he was about to say would not be easy. David looked down at Mary Kate with apologetic blue eyes. He smiled half-heartedly, his beautiful face looking worn by the sands of time. Mary Kate tried to smile, her mouth obeyed, but her eyes did not. David could understand her pain, so he took her hand in his.

"I can't imagine what you all must have been through," Captain Rostron began. "Our crew will ensure that we can make each and everyone of you as comfortable as possible on our way to New York."

The captain hung his head as tears welled in his eyes. He squeezed them shut and continued to talk. "Let's pray. God Almighty, You have made the Heaven and the Earth. Give us comfort that we may live and pray for the lost souls of *Titanic*, that they have found You in heaven."

Sniffles could be heard from every corner of the grand room.

"Please, Lord, let us continue our journey safely, and give us peace and touch us with Your comfort that only You can give." Captain Rostron looked up at the ceiling as if he was expecting God to appear. Then he turned and left as the several hundred that were there stood silently, still trying to comprehend what befell them just the night before.

Mary Kate and David spent the rest of the time on *Carpathia* together. They tried to keep their conversations lighthearted and happy, but somehow they always turned back to the ship and her doom. Mary Kate would quietly sing to David, and he would hold her and wipe away her tears when the silence of the night allowed terror to reclaim her thoughts.

As the *Carpathia* pulled into New York, Mary Kate and David promised to not forget what happened to them and to stay in touch.

"Mary Kate, I'm sorry."

"You didn't cause my troubles, David, I did." Mary Kate looked sadly away as they stood on the deck of the rescue ship in the driving rain. Feeling as if the black cloud had followed them all the way from the North Atlantic, the pair shivered under the black umbrella together that David held.

"Please stay in touch, you know where I'll be." David smiled at her weakly, and his handsome blue eyes were filled with sadness, even though he smiled. Mary Kate nodded weakly as they stepped off of *Carpathia* on to the dock.

Pier 54 was full of people and cars, all thronged together to see the straggling leftover victims of *Titanic*. News reached the rest of the world fast about *Titanic*'s fate. Even if all these people cared, it could not change the fact that so many were lost.

Mary Kate felt lost in the bustle, she was pushed and bumped against people running to their loved ones, or running away as fast as they could from the crowd to seek privacy.

Looking around anxiously, Mary Kate lost sight of David in the clamorous crowd. Where should she go? What should she do? She had been cared for and directed where to go the last few days, and now she was lost in a sea of unknown people!

She had nothing with her but her body. She had no money. She looked around helplessly as the screams and cries created enough noise to fill New York Harbor for hours. She watched people reunite with loved ones and was jealous of their reunions.

She found a crewman standing with a clipboard and an umbrella near the exit.

"Pardon me...." Mary Kate tapped him on the arm. "Have all *Titanic* passengers been accounted for?" she asked quietly.

"Most, Miss, how about you? Are you a survivor?" he asked with as much vivacity of someone doing his job could do. Unsure of how to answer, Mark Kate looked down at her feet. She believed she wasn't a survivor, she could die of heartbreak at any moment!

"No, not me. There are two I am looking for." She looked at the man hesitantly, not meeting his eyes with the shame of her lie.

"The first one is Matthew, Matthew Burnes. Travelling in first class." She searched the young man's expression.

The man looked at the list and after a few moments looked at Mary Kate.

"What's the other name?"

Mary Kate stammered. "Patrick McKinney, traveling third-third class."

Again, the man looked regretfully at Mary Kate.

"Sorry, Miss, neither name." The man shook his head. Mary Kate thanked him and smiled apologetically. Tears stung her eyes as she turned around to face the still crowded pier. An older woman touched Mary Kate's shoulders.

The first class lady smiled at her warmly. "What's your trouble, dear?"

"I have nothing. No money, my brother's gone, my first love is gone...." Mary Kate began to sob tearfully.

The woman held Mary Kate to her frame as she shook with

sobs. "Well, there's a lot of people like that, you are not alone. I have a hotel room tonight where I am putting some others up, you are welcome to stay there until we can figure out what to do." The woman seemed to remain surprisingly calm in the light of the disaster.

"Thank you." The woman held on to Mary Kate's hand as they trailed through the crowd. Looking up, Mary Kate recognized a face in the crowd and pondered where she had seen that face before. A stern face, it was that of William! Mary Kate looked quickly away. He couldn't recognize her, because he had never seen her before, but he looked the same as he had in his picture with his stern face and wild eyes. She wondered if she should give in and go with him, but fate had been cruel and kind at the same time! Aunt Opal stood next to him and looked about nervously. She had not seen Mary Kate since she was a little girl, so she could also escape her stare. Mary Kate followed the lady wearing the black fur coat and wide-brimmed hat closely. She got past William and Aunt Opal, who would think Mary Kate perished with others on the ship. Anxiety gripped her as she headed forward with her second chance.

Chapter 13

Mary Kate stood on the threshold of the large home. Philadelphia had turned out to be a much larger city than she anticipated, but she knew she had to find Matthew's family. They were all that was left of her former life. She couldn't go back to Ireland and face her father. Even though she had seen William on the pier, she couldn't carry out her duty to marry him. It was just better that they all thought she was dead and gone down with Patrick.

It was the first week of May, nearly three weeks since the disaster. The nice lady that helped Mary Kate the first night in America had given her some money to start off with. It was enough to buy Mary Kate a train ticket to Philadelphia, and she was lucky enough to find someone to let her stay in a downtown hotel this last week doing laundry and housekeeping to earn her keep. No one ever knew she had been on *Titanic* or what Mary Kate had been through, and she planned to keep it that way.

Now, Mary Kate's stomach turned in knots as she was about to see Matthew's family. She knocked hesitantly on the large red door. A young maid about Mary Kate's age answered.

"May I help you, Miss?"

"I would like to speak to Mr. or Mrs. Burnes, please," Mary Kate said timidly, clasping her hands in front of her.

The young girl was curious after looking at Mary Kate's appearance. "Is it the maid position?"

"Yes," Mary Kate lied. It might be the only way she would

get inside.

"Just a moment." The young lady bustled away in her black and white uniform.

Mary Kate stood in the foyer of the grand home. She was overcome with awe, standing in the place where Matthew's presence was near.

She heard the clicking of heels on the tile floor and turned around. Mary Kate stared, and her jaw gaped open in awe. The man standing there looked exactly like Matthew, only with a few more wrinkles around his eyes. Mary Kate's knees became weak, and she feared she would faint.

Mr. Burnes noticed her turning pale and ran over to her just as she started to fall.

"Flossie!" he cried to the young maid.

Charles Burnes held the young lady in his arms as Flossie ran back in. She gasped and ran back to the kitchen to get some water. Mary Kate made a few unintelligible noises and looked up at Mr. Burnes, who still held on to her. When she looked in his eyes, she noticed they were the same green hue as Matthew's.

Flossie ran back in with some water and sprinkled it on Mary Kate's face. Sputtering, Mary Kate finally could stand on her own. She wiped her face with the white towel Flossie handed her.

"Thank you," she muttered wearily.

"Come, let's go in my office." Mr. Burnes led Mary Kate down the large oak-paneled hallway into a large room filled top to bottom with books and papers.

"I am so grateful, you probably don't want to talk to me now, do you?" Mary Kate slumped wearily into a green leather chair in front of the large desk and her teeth chattered from nervousness.

"No, actually, I made up the maid position to keep Flossie quiet. I knew she would talk, and, well, it doesn't matter. I figured you would be coming soon." Mr. Burnes settled back in his chair. Mary Kate looked away from his gaze, shaking her head with confusion.

"Do you want to know how I know about you, Mary Kate?" Mr. Burnes asked sheepishly.

Mary Kate's cheeks turned red. How did he know her?

Mr. Burnes opened his top desk drawer and fished out a slip of paper. He slid it across the desk to Mary Kate. She swallowed hard and looked up at Mr. Burnes. He motioned for her to go ahead.

Mr. Burnes asked hesitantly, "I'm sorry, I did not even think. Can you read?" Mary Kate nodded slowly, and quivered when she looked at the starchy white paper. It beckoned her to read it.

Mary Kate trembled as she unfolded the paper and began to pour over its words. It was a telegram. Sent from the *Titanic*.

April 14, 1912

Mother and Father,

I need to tell you something you might not accept. I'm in love with a girl. Bringing her to Philadelphia. Name is Mary Kate McKinney. Treat her with respect and dignity. More later. Be home soon.
Love,

Matthew.

Mary Kate closed her eyes and pursed her lips to fight back tears. She sighed morosely.

"Are you going to be all right?" Mr. Burnes asked. Mary Kate shrugged her trembling shoulders and sighed.

"I lost my only son. I can't tell you how painful that is," Mr. Burnes continued, and Mary Kate stood up weakly. Her blue eyes were glassy with tears, and Mr. Burnes looked away from her sad face for fear he would cry, too. He couldn't imagine the tragedy she had been through.

Mary Kate gasped and burst out of the office and through the great oak halls. She flew by Flossie, who clucked and shook her head. Flossie thought sadly that it wouldn't be the first girl Mr. Burnes had sent away in tears.

Mr. Burnes came charging down the hall.

"Flossie, stop her!" he cried, pointing at Mary Kate.

"OH!" Flossie cried, and she ran after Mary Kate. She ran past Mary Kate and blocked the door with her small body. She was terribly confused.

Sobbing uncontrollably when Mr. Burnes reached her, Mary Kate stopped trying to escape and fell to the first step, her face buried in her hands. Flossie gaped, open-jawed, and looked at Mr. Burnes with questioning blue eyes.

Mary Kate looked up through her tears and saw a pale white figure standing on the staircase, clutching her frilly white housecoat together with frail hands.

"Has she come, Charles?"

Chapter 14

Mrs. Burnes came down the large staircase, clutching the rail all the way down. Mary Kate sniffled as the pale woman descended the staircase and helped the young girl stand up.

"Dear child!" The woman stroked Mary Kate's soft white cheek.

"I don't understand, he said that you–" Mary Kate began hesitantly, wanting to tell them of Matthew's reservations of bringing home his poor Irish girl.

"Don't talk. Flossie, get some tea and meet us in the parlor. We'll talk there." Mrs. Burnes held Mary Kate's arm and led her through the grand oak halls once again into a refreshingly bright room, filled with comfortable furniture and large ornate drapes. On one end of the large room was a stone fireplace, and the older woman led her to a comfortable red satin-covered chair in front of it.

Mrs. Burnes sat politely on a small couch parallel Mary Kate, so she could look at her. Mary Kate looked up at the walls and gasped. There was a beautiful painted portrait on the wall. Four girls and one boy stared back at her. The young girls in the portrait were all beautiful and blond like their mother. She swallowed the lump in her throat. The boy was Matthew, but as a little boy of maybe four or five.

"I'm sorry, dear. Oh God!" Mrs. Burnes sobbed pitifully. Mary Kate could do nothing to help her. Realizing that Mrs. Burnes had lost her only son, Mary Kate felt helpless, since she had also lost her first love. Things had happened so fast, and they blurred her memory as she thought of everything she had been through in the last few weeks.

"I'm sorry I cannot help you," Mary Kate finally spoke.

"No one can help us." Mrs. Burnes tried to compose herself as Flossie brought in the tea. Mrs. Burnes poured herself and Mary Kate each some of the steaming liquid in little china cups adorned with dainty yellow roses.

"I suppose Mr. Burnes shared the telegram with you." Mary Kate slurped the hot tea graciously. Mrs. Burnes nodded, setting her tea on the small oak table in front of her.

"I don't know what to even say to you." Replying honestly, Mary Kate looked away from the beautiful older woman and her intent blue gaze.

"Matthew was a very good boy, but very headstrong. He would fight hard for anything her believed in. The fact that he had the foresight to send us a telegram meant that he loved you, and he was going to try to break us in."

"Break you in? Are you ashamed of me?" Mary Kate exclaimed nervously, but she had to know.

"Absolutely not!" Mrs. Burnes acted shocked. Mary Kate was confused of the Burnesed' actions. Matthew and her brother, Patrick, had both acted as if the differences in Mary Kate and Matthew's status was the end of the world, but now Mrs. Burnes acted hurt, as if anyone could ever think of it!

"I'm sorry, Madam, but I think Matthew thought it would be more of an issue."

"And perhaps it would have been if he lived...." Mrs. Burnes picked up her tea again and trailed off.

"I did care for your son very much." Mary Kate smiled, though she still sensed something was amiss.

"I know, and he must have enjoyed your company, too. But we are glad you came."

"Are you?"

"Oh, yes, I just wanted to see you. To know my dear sweet

Matthew in his last few days was close to someone I can touch and see and–" Mrs. Burnes burst into sobs again. This time Mary Kate jumped over to the couch and put her arms around the hysterical woman. Mary Kate had felt like this woman so many times in the last few weeks. She went from being able to deal with the enormity of the tragedy to maniacal sobs. She could relate to Mrs. Burnes' tragedy, yet she could really be of no comfort to the distraught woman.

"Perhaps I'd better go." Mary Kate stood up.

"No, no, please don't let me scare you off with my hysterics." Mrs. Burnes sniffled and tried to smooth over her wild blond hair coming loose from its pins that secured it in its place.

"What more good can I be to you?" Mary Kate eyed the woman carefully. It was nice to be so close to Matthew's family. She felt like she had somewhere to belong after the shipwreck and all its trials.

"You could stay with us, dear," Mrs. Burnes mentioned, her melancholy attitude suddenly changing.

"Oh, I don't know, I wouldn't feel right about staying here for nothing."

"Well, then, you could cook on the nights Robert isn't here, and clean with Flossie. You could have your own room and–" Mrs. Burnes continued, quickly becoming more cheerful, in a way that was frankly false.

"Well, I suppose I could stay for a little while then," Mary Kate agreed, and soon she was escorted to a room next to the kitchen.

"Flossie!" Mrs. Burnes knocked on the large wooden door. Mary Kate looked at Mrs. Burnes with an expression of shock in her blue eyes. It sure hadn't taken long for Mrs. Burnes to take Mary Kate up on her offer.

Flossie pulled open the door with rude abruptness and stood stunned when Mrs. Burnes shoved the young Irish woman inside. Mary Kate was as startled as Flossie when she went flying into the dark room, a little oil lamp the only light. There were no windows in the room, and two small cots with a small table made out of scrap wood between them. There were hooks in the wall where some clothes hung, and a hat stand in the corner. It was more like a closet or a pantry than a room!

Mary Kate sighed as Mrs. Burnes shut the door. It seemed she cast her away and wanted nothing more to do with her. Flossie smiled at Mary Kate and sat down on her bed. Mary Kate sat on the other small cot, that was as hard as a lump of coal. She thought she was poor when she lived in Ireland, but her bed there was made of feathers at least, and a little bit softer.

"I see you got the position." Flossie smiled.

"I don't know what I just agreed to." Mary Kate laughed.

Flossie extended her very small, very white hand. "I'm Flossie Bennett."

"Mary Kate McKinney." Mary Kate smiled and shook the other young woman's hand firmly.

"I don't know what all that was about earlier in the foyer, and you don't have to tell me, but Mr. and Mrs. Burnes have been looking for another servant since Thomas perished," Flossie continued talking at a harried pace.

Mary Kate swallowed the lump in her throat. Flossie had no idea Mary Kate had been on *Titanic* with Matthew, and that she knew Thomas as well.

She simply nodded and listened to Flossie begin to explain what she would be doing for the Burnes to earn her keep.

Mary Kate kneeled down in the large cathedral. This was the first time she had been at church since *Titanic*, and she still felt a little ill from the tragedy of it all. She knew she had to get back into a normal routine, or she would lose control of all her life.

As she prayed, she could hear footsteps approaching on the marble floor that echoed through the massive building and off the stone walls.

"Oh, good day to you, Miss." Mary Kate looked up into the face of a chubby white-haired priest adorned with his black robes and collar.

Mary Kate said shyly, "Good day."

"Are you new to Philadelphia?" the priest asked, kneeling down in the pew with her.

"Yes, you could say that."

"Hmmm. You sound like you have a little bit of an accent. I bet you are Irish." The priest smiled, speaking in his own Irish drawl.

Mary Kate smiled. "Well, yes, you could say that too."

"I'm Father Murphy." He extended his thick hand to her.

Mary Kate took it and gleefully smiled. "I'm Mary Kate McKinney."

"Well, if that isn't a fine Irish name, I don't know what is." The cherry cheeked man laughed. Mary Kate couldn't help but chuckle at the man's demeanor.

"Thank you."

"You seem sad, my dear. Do you need to talk about something?"

"Well, I'm just very confused right now … and it's such a long story…." Mary Kate sighed. She felt relieved. Father Murphy, it seemed, had very good intuition.

"I have time for a long story. There's no mass 'til noon. Besides, I like a good story." The cherub-faced man smiled genuinely and sat back in the pew.

"Well, it started in April. I came to America on *Titanic*–"

Father Murphy interrupted. "Mercy me!"

"Yes, it was awful!" Mary Kate cried out in tears. She still could not believe sometimes that it actually happened to her. That she watched it happen and *Titanic* itself seemed like it was

121

to blame more than the iceberg. Father Murphy hugged her tightly to his round frame. He hushed her and promised it would be all right and that God does things for a reason.

"I'm sorry." Mary Kate sniffled.

"Well, don't apologize. You are not to blame for anything." Father Murphy felt so terrible for the young girl. Mary Kate continued to tell him about Matthew and how she felt responsible for the wreck and the perished lives and the guilt she carried with her. She felt she could never recover from never being able to face her brothers and father again.

"That is not your fault. No one did that to punish you," Father Murphy affirmed.

"Are you sure God doesn't hate me?" Mary Kate asked with red eyes.

"No, no ... sweet child. God loves you, otherwise would you be here? With me in this church? Sometimes we can't understand why God does the things He does. Just trust in him, Mary Katherine. Just trust him." Father Murphy struck his breast with his hand.

Mary Kate sighed and nodded.

Father Murphy resumed a kneeling position next to her in the pew. He took her hand in his and gave her an adoring smile. "Let us say the Lord's prayer together," he said plainly, and as Mary Kate recited the words to the familiar prayer, she felt absolved of a million things she had carried with her since the wreck of the most famous ship in history.

A long length black dress with long sleeves, complete with a white apron and cap, became Mary Kate's new attire. She felt outlandish and silly wearing it. Her own clothes, though bland and plain, hung on one of the hooks in her room. She couldn't bear to lose them; they were all she had left of her *Titanic* trip. Her patchwork blue dress that she wore the day her and Matthew first kissed. She would keep the tatters until she was an old lady to remind her of that fateful day!

Trapped away in a corner closet by the kitchen, how horrid it was to be stowed away in her and Flossie's room. It hurt her feelings that the Burnes were doing this to her. The woman their son had loved was being made a servant. The Burnes ordered her around angrily, and Mary Kate resented being here. Where else could she go? She had no money. Had these people no love in their heart? Mary Kate felt this was the only way she could keep Matthew alive in her memory. She was working for room and board only, and she was made to scrub on her hands and knees and reach places and clean things twice in a row if Mrs. Burnes felt the urge to make her do so. Mary Kate didn't mind working; it helped to keep her mind off of everything she had been through. She minded being treated cruelly, especially by someone she wanted so desperately to love her.

"It's time, I guess," Flossie said to Mary Kate one rainy Tuesday morning. Mary Kate wrinkled her eyebrows at Flossie's sad expression.

"Time for what?"

"To clean Matthew's room."

Mary Kate gulped. She was led to believe that Flossie knew nothing of Mary Kate's travels. "Oh." She carried on with the charade that she knew nothing, but secretly Mary Kate did not want Flossie to say the words aloud. She did not want to hear stories and assumptions of what happened that dark April night.

Flossie bit her lower lip. "I just don't think I can do it."

"I-I can do it," Mary Kate stuttered and she continued to play stupid.

"Oh, would you mind, Mary? I would be forever grateful." Flossie always abbreviated the name to "Mary." Mary Kate thought it endearing and unique of her new and only friend. Mary Kate had already known which room was Matthew's. It was the room at the top of the stairs that never opened, like someone was trying to keep the spirits from escaping. Flossie explained anyway which room was Matthew's, and Mary Kate slowly ascended the staircase, the wood creaking underneath her feet.

Opening the door hesitantly, Mary Kate for an instant almost believed that Matthew might be on the other side. Her breath left her as she stepped inside the dark room and the familiar smell of mold and cobwebs hit her like a train full of fumes. It had been several months since the Burnes had been in this room. She was shoved away in a corner and closed off from the world; much the way that this room had sat empty since *Titanic* sank. The shades were nearly closed completely, and only a thin sash of daylight peeked through. Mary Kate opened the shades to reveal the overcast sky. Her heart was pounding in her chest as she glided the feather duster over the windowsills.

Matthew's things were in neat and tidy piles. There was a stack of books on an ornate shelf in the corner by the closet. Mary Kate slowly approached them and caressed them lightly. Tears formed in the corner of her eyes as she lifted each book from its place to dust under it. She imagined Matthew reading each one and carefully setting it here to rest. Perhaps he would return and read it again, or so he thought. Mary Kate shook her head from her morbid thoughts. The dust was mingling with the salt in her tears and forcing them to sting. She wiped her eyes with her sleeve and continued on to the dresser. She knew that peeking was something that good maids did not do. That was what Flossie had told Mary Kate the first week she had shadowed her to learn her duties. Mary Kate couldn't resist here in this room where Matthew's presence filled every corner. Mary Kate opened the top dresser drawer and peeked inside. A lot of his clothes remained there, folded and stacked neatly. Mary Kate continued on to the next drawer and the next, dusting all as she went. She stood before the bed. The feather pillow still had a dent from Matthew's head in it. She lifted it from the bed and gently sniffed it. It smelled vaguely of his soapy scent, and Mary Kate hugged the pillow to her body, tears rolling gently from her eyes. She slapped it gently to fluff it and smoothed the covers with her hand, her skin aching to touch the spot where he had once lain to sleep. She wanted to cry out loud! She wanted to scream the truth to Flossie and Matthew's parents. She wanted to run and never look back, screaming until she had it out of her system. Instead, she sighed and picked up her feather duster, managing to drive out the spider's webs that were hanging in the corners. She took one long last look at Matthew's things and left the room with her head hung low.

"Mary?" Flossie was waiting at the next bedroom over. Mary Kate quickly raised her head, and her stomach fluttered. Had Flossie heard her crying?

Mary Kate smiled weakly. "It still needs a good sweeping."

"But it's done?" Flossie's eyes darted away, and Mary Kate simply nodded.

"Yes."

"Thank you, Mary."

"Was no trouble at all." Mary Kate turned and went down the stairs, relieved that she had gone to his room. She would always have wondered what it contained if her friend had not been too afraid to clean it.

Mary Kate stood in the great comfortable living room she had sat with Mrs. Burnes in her first day here. The day she first thought the Burnes were going to accept her. Matthew and Patrick had been right! How could she think things were going to be better than they told her? They weren't! They were incredibly awful.

Mary Kate's mind drifted as she came to the painting of Matthew and his sisters. She stopped in front of it for a moment and looked into Matthew's eyes. She didn't know who the artist was, but he or she had magnificently captured Matthew's green eyes, that haunted her heart.

"Oh, Matthew!" Mary Kate clutched her heart and fell on the hardwood floor on her knees. She did not cry, only sighed with torment. She couldn't believe he was gone! It just couldn't be real. Yesterday having to clean Matthew's room had made her feel so close to him, but now today she realized she was even further away from him. She thought about Matthew and what he had said to her just before the ship hit the iceberg. He was going to take her on that ship again someday. Now it was all so far away and strange. None of it would ever come true now, none of it! To see his face just once more, or to look in his beautiful eyes again! She felt so hopeless, she could never expect to be happy again, this was her punishment for disobeying her father and her family! But she had to believe Father Murphy. God was not punishing her.

Mary Kate could hear footsteps coming, and she quickly got to her feet, continuing to dust. Flossie came running in the room with a smile on her pale face.

"Guess what?" she cried excitedly.

"What?" Mary Kate asked soberly, she could feel no reason for excitement.

"The Burnes, they are going to have a party!" Flossie cried with the inflamed expectations of a young girl. Perhaps she had never had her hopes dashed or lost a love. To her it was the dawning of something glamorous.

Mary Kate smiled and tried to be happy for her new friend.

Chapter 15

Things were beginning to get underway at the Burnes' Philadelphia mansion. Mary Kate and Flossie were ordered that week to scrub in every nook and cranny. All six servants were on duty, and all the lights were lit tonight as the guests began to appear.

Flossie and Mary Kate stood in the large upstairs window watching behind the curtain.

"I see the most beautiful ball gowns from up here!" Flossie smiled at Mary Kate.

Mary Kate smiled wearily. "I'm sure they are most elegant."

"Oh indeed!" Flossie giggled, her blond curls poked out from under her white cap.

"Oh, look! Look at this one! That's Mr. and Mrs. Burnes' oldest daughter, Claire!" Flossie shook Mary Kate's arm excitedly.

"Yes she is very pretty." Mary Kate peered over Flossie's shoulders.

"Oh, all the Burnes' daughters are beautiful, but you should've met their son. Now he was a charmer!" Flossie giggled like a little girl. Mary Kate choked back tears. Flossie still had no idea why Mary Kate had come to Philadelphia.

"Such a shame Master Burnes passed on," Flossie continued. "He died heroically, I'm sure. On *Titanic*." Flossie made it sound as if dying on the wreck of *Titanic* was something to be envious of. Mary Kate sadly realized that Flossie had no idea that Mary Kate had stood on the deck of that great vessel, or that she had watched it founder from a lifeboat. Flossie also did not now that Mary Kate knew what a charmer Matthew was, and that she had kissed her heroic Master Burnes!

Mary Kate excused herself as Flossie remained glued to the window, watching the arriving guests with naïve admiration. Salty tears formed in Mary Kate's eyes as she hid herself in a closet near the staircase.

When Mary Kate felt she could control herself, she exited the small closet and made her way downstairs to begin dinner service. She daydreamed that perhaps if Matthew had lived, she would be descending the staircase in a splendorous glittering ball gown. She would stand next to Matthew's sisters and be admired by the maids. Matthew would take her by the arm and smile his handsome bright smile and escort her to dinner.

Mary Kate stopped daydreaming when Mr. Burnes gave her a sharp look. He could always tell when she was not at full attention. *Why do I allow myself to be tortured?* Mary Kate asked herself as she made her way into the large kitchen to finish preparing the lavish meal.

Dinner went smoothly. The meal that she and Robert, the cook, had prepared was loved by all. Mr. Burnes did his share of bossing Mary Kate around, like always. He knew she would do whatever he wanted, so he took advantage of it. Mary Kate could feel Matthew's two sisters that attended the gala staring at her. She was sure their mother or father had told them about her *Titanic* adventures with their brother, and it made Mary Kate's blood boil. What happened between her and Matthew was so sacred, but it was being made a farce of by his family. Mary Kate silently wondered what Matthew would think of all this. Deep inside, she knew what he would think.

Mary Kate stood in the kitchen. Robert, who cooked for the Burnes, was standing near the stove smoking a cigarette. He wiped his large black hands on his apron.

"Well, do you think they liked it?" he asked his young friend.

"Oh, yes, Robert. Everyone absolutely raved about it," Mary Kate told him as she filled the kettle with hot water to start the dishes.

"Mary Kate, I've seen a lot of things in my life." The black man, about fifty years of age, smiled at her, his white teeth gleaming brilliantly.

"Oh?" Mary Kate continued filling up the large kettle. She looked up at Robert, her eyes expressing her desire to hear what he would say next.

"Find me, dear, if you wish to talk." Robert proceeded to the back door to his outside quarters. He never offered any more insight into his comment.

"Good night, Robert." Mary Kate watched the large man stroll off despondently.

Somehow, she got the feeling that Robert knew more than he let on. He was always more reserved and quiet around her than the others were. At first Mary Kate thought Robert didn't speak to her much because she was new, but her intuition told her that he knew more than he let on, and his warm brown eyes expressed more than his words ever could.

Mary Kate poured the hot water in the sink, her hands wrinkled from soaking in the water. She was alone in the kitchen now, and it was silent. She could hear far laughter and music from the ballroom. Her mind wandered, and she closed her eyes. She remembered standing on the deck of *Titanic* and closing her eyes. Hearing the same distant music and laughter. Suddenly, she was thankful to have her hands submersed in the warm water. She could no longer touch water without thinking of the icy cold waters of the North Atlantic and the fate it had brought her to.

The door to the kitchen swung open with a loud creak, and Mary Kate did not turn around. Instead she returned quickly to her task, in case it were Mr. Burnes.

"Pardon me, but I was wondering if I could hear an Irish lullaby?"

Mary Kate whipped around to the sound of a familiar voice. "David!" she cried, and without thinking, she wrapped her soapy arms around his neck as he stepped near to her.

"I thought that was you!" David laughed, small wrinkles forming at the corners of his heavenly blue eyes.

Mary Kate released her hold and dried her hands on her white apron. "I'm so glad to see you."

"I didn't recognize you with your duds there." David pointed to her black and white maid outfit, complete with white cap that tried its best to contain her wild auburn curls.

"Oh, you!" Mary Kate laughed.

"I could never mistake those pretty eyes for another though."

"Well, look at you, though, don't you like nice!" Mary Kate laughed, remarking on David's handsome black tuxedo.

"Yes, smart, isn't it?" David laughed warmly, looking down at his sharp dress attire.

"So what brings you to Philadelphia?" Mary Kate asked, surprised at her good fortune of seeing David again so soon.

"Oh, Virginia and Matthew's grandfather, Mr. Brown. He's trying to play matchmaker with me and some young debutante." David laughed again. Mary Kate's stomach leapt involuntarily, though she didn't recognize it as jealousy.

"Anyone interesting?" Mary Kate queried, trying to be happy for David going on with his life.

"Not a one, they are all pretty, but not much up here!" David tapped on his slicked dark locks as young Mary Kate laughed.

"Well, they would have to be pretty smart to keep up with you." She smiled.

"Thank you. I trust all is well with you?" David said, though he knew things were not well for her.

"Oh, yes, fine," Mary Kate lied. The truth was she hated it

in Philadelphia! Her eyes gave her away.

"Mary Kate, please don't say that when I know it's not true." David hushed her when she started to object, "I saw the way Mr. Burnes treated you at dinner! You can't live like this, Mary Kate. This is exactly what Matthew did not want for you!" David's warm eyes were sincere with worry, and his deep voice was calm and polite. Mary Kate could feel tears springing to her eyes.

"I know, but what am I to do?" she begged him, hoping he would find an answer.

"Come with me, to Iowa. I can pay your train fare. You can't stay here. You will die from the pressure and the heartbreak that surrounds you." David took Mary Kate's soggy hand and kissed it tenderly.

Mary Kate looked at him sadly.

"Please?" David asked her again, and he raised his eyebrows, expecting a reply.

Mary Kate nodded somberly, and David shoved thirty dollars in her hand.

"Come to Iowa whenever you're ready. I must go." David gave her a pleading look before disappearing out the swinging kitchen door.

Mary Kate's heart sank. He was right. She was here clinging on to memories of someone she couldn't bring back from the dead, no matter how hard she tried to keep his memory alive! She was subjecting herself to the Burnes' cruel love. They were supposed to love her for Matthew's sake, instead they had made her a slave. It was exactly what Matthew had *not* wanted for her!

Mary Kate resolved to do what David asked her. She would start over in Iowa and find something there. She could no longer be a slave to a family that was so cold.

After finishing the dishes, Mary Kate returned to her "closet." She had almost changed out of her sweaty uniform when she remembered what Robert said. He had told her to find him later if she needed to talk. There was no better time than now after David had come to her tonight. She would have to make a decision. Stay or go.

Mary Kate quietly left the kitchen through the back door. Her feet swished through the grass as she made her way towards the small glowing light from inside Robert's small brick quarters. As she approached, she became nervous. She knocked quietly.

"Robert!" she whispered through the large keyhole in the door.

The large cook opened the door and ushered her inside quickly. "I'm glad you came, girl," Robert said in a hushed tone.

"If it's all right, I'd like to talk to you." Mary Kate wrung her hands nervously. If Mr. Burnes caught her here, she would get both her and Robert in trouble.

"Well, sit down." Robert motioned to a small chair by the bed that had been cobbled together with small leftover pieces of boards. His small brick hut was only about as big as the closet that Mary Kate and Flossie shared, and it only had space for a small bed and a chair and a small oil lamp. There was a small wood stove on the opposite end from where the bed was.

"Robert, I need to tell you something. I feel like you are the only one who may understand." Mary Kate sat on the chair, and her eyes followed him as he sat on the bed, facing her.

"I think I know what you might say."

"You do?"

"Yes, I do. Listen, girl. I know about you and Matthew." As Robert said it, Mary Kate's breath escaped her like a bursting bubble. She had suspected he might know more than he let on.

"Why are they doing this to me, then?" Mary Kate's eyes began to glisten with tears.

"I don't know, little girl. I know that the mornin' that

telegram came, we had already heard of the wreck. Mr. and Mrs. were so inconsolable; someone else had to read it. Flossie can't read, so I had to read it." Robert's eyes were full of sorrow as he relayed his story, and he cast his sad eyes down at the floor.

"I loved Matthew so much. I don't know why I even came here." Mary Kate also stared blankly at the dirt floor.

"Because you wanted to be close to him again. Matthew was very special. I've worked for the Burnes since the war. When I moved up here after bein' freed, I guess I didn't know what else to do but cook. So Mr. Burnes' father actually hired me, and I guess I just figured it was right to stay around." Robert chuckled, his eyes showing his wisdom.

"So you've known Matthew since he was a baby?"

"Oh my, yes! He was always different from the others, too. He liked people. He never once forgot to tell me "good mornin'" or ask how I was doin'. Servant or whoever, he loved everyone. You know what I'm sayin'? He looked into a person's heart, not their outward kind."

Mary Kate swallowed the lump in her throat. That was exactly what Matthew could do, see the heart in every person.

"But girl, you need to get on with your life. You can't stay here to try to hold on to him. He's gone. He's gone...." Robert's brown eyes flooded as he whispered it over and over. Mary Kate grabbed Robert's large black hand. She patted it softly.

"Thank you, Robert. If it weren't for you helping me to see that, I might have to spend the rest of my life living in a closet, dreaming of some thing that won't come true."

"No matter how hard we pray, Miss. It won't come true. Get out of here while you still can. It's too late for me."

"I will, Robert." Mary Kate's stomach twisted in knots. It wouldn't be easy to break free, but she had to in order to save herself from the painful memories.

Chapter 16

Mary Kate woke up Sunday morning, feeling a little renewed. David was right, and it had taken him to point out to her what she already knew. She had seen her chains to Matthew's family as jewels for Matthew's sake. The butterflies in her stomach were out of control, but she would have to tell them she was leaving.

Visiting with Robert had also helped Mary Kate see the torment she had subjected herself to. The Burnes had taken advantage of her innocence. Robert understood her deep feelings, and also why now she must go. Mary Kate felt so good just to be able to tell someone about Matthew, she had been keeping it inside for too long now. She had lost track of time, and it was to be her birthday next week. She had let her emotions keep her away from her life since *Titanic* went down.

When Mary Kate woke Sunday morning, she did not put on her maid's uniform. She stood in front of Flossie and gently shook her shoulder to waken her.

"What is it, Mary?" Flossie slowly awakened.

"Flossie, I have to tell you something. I am leaving today." Mary Kate started to become teary.

Flossie jumped out of her bed, her long blond curls askew from sleeping on them. "Oh, no! You can't! I can't survive here without you!"

"I'm sorry, but I have to. You know the first day I came?" Flossie nodded.

"Well, the Burnes were told I was coming here. By telegram.

From Matthew." Flossie's blue eyes widened in curiosity.

"I met Matthew on *Titanic*, Flossie. We were in love and to be together when we got to America, but now that's all changed. I came here to hold on to Matthew's memory, but now I see I've just been played a joke on by the Burnes," Mary Kate explained. Flossie continued to listen to her friend's story.

"Why didn't you tell me sooner instead of keeping all that heartbreak inside you?" Flossie asked Mary Kate, and she hugged her friend.

"I thought I could bring Matthew back by living here. I thought I could keep a little piece of him in my heart." Mary Kate clutched her breast as she tried to keep the tears from streaming from her blue eyes.

"Well, Mary. I wish I were as brave as you. I may never be able to leave here, because I have no family left. So, you ought to have this." Flossie reached down by the table and fished around in her maid's dress pocket that was hanging on a hook above her bed. She handed Mary Kate the gold and ruby ring that had belonged to Matthew!

"Oh, dear God! Flossie, how did you come by it?" Mary Kate cried happily.

"I found it on the floor under your bed. It must have fallen out of your dress pocket when you were made to wear that dreadful thing." Flossie laughed. She pointed to Mary Kate's maid uniform still hanging above the other cot. Mary Kate chuckled and reflected on the ruby for a moment. She had forgotten it was in her pocket. It had been with her since that fateful Sunday on *Titanic*. It had made it through the scrape with Ryan, the lifeboat, the pier, and the Philadelphia trip. It was meant to be with her as a symbol of Matthew, and the love she had for him that would never die.

"Thank you." Mary Kate hugged her friend, and they said their good-byes.

As Mary Kate exited the room, Flossie quickly got dressed.

She wanted to make it to the breakfast table in time to hear the Burnes' reaction!

Mary Kate hesitantly walked into the dining room. Mr. Burnes looked up from his coffee. He angrily set down his paper, his small lips pursed tightly.

"Why aren't you dressed yet?" he demanded angrily.

"Because I'm not working today." Mary Kate mustered all the courage she had to face the cruel man. Her heart was pounding a mile a minute.

"What?" Mr. Burnes was shocked. "Go back and get dressed before Mrs. Burnes gets down here! Stop all this nonsense!"

"The young lady said she's not working today!" Robert stepped out from behind the kitchen door.

"Robert, you get your ass back in there!" Mr. Burnes pointed angrily to the kitchen, standing up out of his chair.

"Stop it!" Mary Kate yelled loudly. Both men looked at the young woman, who was shaking from anger. Mary Kate walked over to Mr. Burnes and looked him in the eyes.

"The first day I came here, I thought you were just like Matthew. You looked like him, and I thought you would be kind and charming like him. I was wrong. You have shown me nothing but disrespect since I walked in this door!" Mary Kate cried.

"Oh." Mr. Burnes realized what he had done and slumped back in the over-stuffed chair.

"I loved your son. I loved him with all my heart, and I believe he felt the same about me. He died, and none of us can ever wish him back! He didn't want me to come here and be your damn slave!" Mary Kate for the first time in her life uttered a sinful word.

"Oh." Mr. Burnes couldn't even talk.

"I can't believe anyone would be so cruel! Didn't you want your son to be happy, for God's sake? I will not work today or any other day for you. I will gladly starve on the street before

I come in this house under your cruel wing again!" Mary Kate turned and left the dining room. She nearly ran into Mrs. Burnes, who had been listening to the whole scene with a gaping jaw outside the dining room. Mary Kate just stared at her harshly before storming out of the front door. Flossie heard the whole thing from the kitchen and giggled under her breath.

Chapter 17

The train station was crowded with people, perhaps returning home after a weekend in the city. Mary Kate nervously walked up to the marble counter.

"Where to?" the grumpy old man behind the counter asked impatiently.

"Iowa," Mary Kate squeaked out.

"Iowa's a big state, honey. Particular destination in mind?" The man twisted the ends of his salt-and-pepper moustache.

"Well, I need to get to Sioux City."

"I think I can arrange that." The man nodded and worked up a ticket for her.

"That's twenty-four dollars." He took her crumpled currency and handed her the ticket through the window, staring at her curiously. "Your train leaves at eleven thirty. That track, all the way to the end." The man pointed and actually smiled, something Mary Kate didn't know he was capable of.

She thanked him and sat on a bench, waiting for eleven thirty. She wished she had one of her books about now, but the painful memory of the last time she touched her book brought goosebumps to her arms. The train ticket took most of the thirty dollars, and she would have only a little bit left for meals. It would be enough to survive. Mary Kate removed her headscarf, setting free her wild auburn hair. She stuck her hands in her pocket and caressed the ruby ring. It was all she had left of Matthew.

Mary Kate's stomach fluttered when she thought about how

she had stood up to Mr. Burnes. He had been cruel to her long enough, and she just couldn't take him treating Robert that way, too. She flushed when she thought about using a swear word. It was not like her. Her brothers and father used those words all the time, but Mary Kate was taught to try to be ladylike and not do that. She wondered what the look on Matthew's face would have been like if he could have seen her stand up to his father like that. She smiled to herself and took the ring out of her pocket.

Mary Kate slipped it on her index finger. The only finger the ring would fit on and stay on. She caressed it, stroking her finger. Matthew's finger and her finger could touch through this special ring. She could feel one with him again.

A thin older woman plopped down on the bench across from Mary Kate. She was dressed lavishly in a bright striped coatdress and dark hat. Wild tentacles of red hair fell from under the hat and stopped just above her shoulders. Mary Kate smiled at her and nodded hello. The older woman smiled, showing no teeth, and folded her gloved hands in her lap.

"So, if I may ask, where are you headed to?" the older woman asked Mary Kate.

"To Iowa."

"Oh, yes, Iowa is pretty, but Colorado is prettier." The woman smiled wider this time.

"I've never been to either," Mary Kate said to herself.

"No, I can tell from your accent probably not," the woman observed of Mary Kate's drawl.

"Well, the last few months have been a very interesting time." Mary Kate looked down at her feet.

"Well, as a matter of fact, I am just returning home from a business trip. I am afraid though that I hoped to be home sooner, but I just couldn't face going home right away, and I had to wait and see if they could find Reggie." The woman's smile turned to a look of disdain, and her voice trailed away.

Mary Kate looked curiously at her; she had a feeling something horrible had also happened to this woman.

"I'm sorry." Mary Kate sadly lowered her head.

"It's not your fault. I've just been through quite an ordeal to get back to America." The older woman looked down at her hands, Mary Kate looked away, afraid she would upset this woman. The woman's green eyes darted nervously over to Mary Kate. The woman's nose was pointy and long, and her cheeks glowed red. Her skin was a little wrinkled, but she held her age well. She looked no older than forty to Mary Kate, though she had given the impression she was older.

Mary Kate sighed and looked down at the ring again. She caressed it tenderly, and the older woman watched the young woman with curiosity. She wondered why she looked so tenderly at the ring.

The older woman asked her. "Are you engaged?"

"No." Mary Kate shook her head, she hadn't realized that the woman had watched her with the ruby ring.

"I'm just curious about your pretty ring there." The older woman pointed and smiled.

"Oh! It's just something that used to belong to a friend of mine." Mary Kate shrugged.

"Oh, I see. A very special friend? Perhaps someone you are going to see in Iowa?"

"Oh, no. This friend was very dear to me, but he is passed away now." Mary Kate did not volunteer any more information than that.

"I'm sorry."

Mary Kate smiled weakly at the woman. "Please, don't be. You didn't know."

"My name is Constance Perkins." The older woman extended her long white hand.

"Mary Kate McKinney." Mary Kate shook the other woman's hand quickly, a little shy.

"I'm sorry to hear about your friend."

"That's all right. You couldn't have known." Mary Kate looked at the ring for a few moments, then slid it off her finger. She held it out to the older woman with a shy grin on her face. Constance smiled, showing her straight white teeth.

Constance's face turned from a smile to a frown when she read the inscription in the ring. Constance dropped shiny ring in Mary Kate's waiting palm.

"I didn't realize. I'm sorry. It must be very hard to lose a friend."

"What I still can't believe was that I only knew him a few days. But from the first moment I met him, we were very close. My brother called it "lovesickness." I don't really know what it was." Mary Kate blinked to keep the tears from coming to her eyes.

Constance sprang up and sat next to Mary Kate on the bench. "You poor thing!" she cried, hugging the young girl tightly. Mary Kate let the woman comfort her, though she didn't want to tell her the whole story.

"Is this someone you had to leave behind in Ireland?" Constance asked the young woman as she still held her.

Mary Kate shook her head.

"I'm sorry" Constance said, "I won't ask you anymore about it." The two women sat silently holding each other for a long time. Constance so missed her children, and Mary Kate so missed her mother at this moment.

Time came to board the train. Constance and Mary Kate thought they would have to part ways but instead discovered they would be on the same train, at least up through Iowa.

"I don't see why we can't sit together if you like." Constance smiled at Mary Kate. Mary Kate nodded weakly and let the older woman help her aboard.

As the train snaked its way westward, Mary Kate looked out the window. The cloak of night was beginning to fall on the darkening landscape. She looked across at her new friend, Constance.

"*Titanic*. I met him on *Titanic*," she confessed.

Constance finally leaned back against the tall seat after Mary Kate recanted her story. She closed her eyes wearily and rubbed them in exhaustion.

"Mary Kate, that is quite a story. Do you mind if I make a confession?"

Mary Kate shook her head as she also settled back in her chair.

"I was on *Titanic*, too. I can't believe this! This is so strange." Constance shook her head in disbelief.

"Tell me, Constance. I had no one to tell for the longest time. Please tell me, it will help."

"Well, my husband, Reggie, is a perfume salesman. We were over in Europe purchasing some samples, and he promised me he would take me back home on the grandest most wonderful ship!" Constance's voice had a hint of sarcasm as she waved her hands in the air to make her point. Mary Kate nodded in agreement to her friend's story, and her mind drifted away to the most romantic night of her life. She could still smell the dusky perfume Virginia had sprayed her with and wondered if it had come from Reggie and Constance.

"We decided that *Titanic* was a once-in-a-lifetime trip for us. We have never been so right in our lives. Listen to me, talking as if Reggie was still here," Constance chided herself, and she looked out the window at the black sky, raising her eyes to the heavens.

"Constance, what happened?"

"Well, as you've said, 'women and children first.' Reggie put me on a boat, and I watched as he helped other women into boats, and as soon as the boat I was in was cut away, I never saw him again." Constance shrugged and shook her head with no expression on her face.

Mary Kate was awed that she could talk about it without shedding a tear. "Why did it happen? I still don't understand." Mary Kate spouted angrily.

"We don't know, we will never know. They had a large inquiry and asked everyone all these questions, but no one still knows."

"Did they find Reggie?"

"Not to my knowledge. I waited and waited and hounded people until I realized I had to go home. If Reggie had lived, he would have found me. I have to be strong and go home and just continue the business and keep it together." Constance bit her lower lip.

"You are strong, Constance!" Mary Kate reached over and grabbed her older friend's hand.

"We both have to be in order to get on with our lives, don't we?"

"Yes, someone has to."

"Your friend, David, that you are going to see. I wish you the best of luck."

"Thank you. Although I do worry that we will always constantly remind each other of it."

"No, you might for a while, and you will always be bonded by it, as you and I will always be. But eventually, *maybe*, our hearts will heal."

"I hope so, I just hate thinking about it all the time."

"I know, it's hard not to."

"I am grateful I found you, Constance."

Constance smiled wearily. "And I, you."

"I couldn't have stood a boring train ride by myself all the way to Iowa."

"It still could be boring!" Constance smirked.

"Not with you, you are never a bore." Mary Kate giggled.

"Well, let's make each other a promise."

"All right."

"Let's agree not to talk about *Titanic* anymore the rest of the trip."

"I agree."

Constance extended her hand to Mary Kate's, and they sealed their deal. The two women smiled at each other. Though fate could be cruel, it could also, at times, be kind as well.

Different stops came and went, and both women would step down from the train and stretch their legs and backs. The few days were long on the train, and it was hard to sleep in the chairs. Mary Kate would rest her head on Constance's shoulder. Constance would smile and pat the young woman's hair tenderly, wishing her children lived closer. Though they promised not to talk about that cursed ship, it still invaded each of their private thoughts often. Not an hour or barely a minute passed when the thought didn't come to mind. There were so many "what ifs." A person could drive herself to madness if they thought about it too much. There was nothing anyone could do, just hope and pray that something like that would never happen again.

The train pulled into a depot in a rough spot of ground just to the west of Des Moines, Iowa. Mary Kate disembarked slowly down the skinny iron steps onto the red brick platform. It was a bright warm day, hotter than any day she had ever seen in Ireland. The trees stood so tall here, and it wasn't quite as green and moist as where she came from. The air here smelled like fresh dirt and steam engine smoke. Mary Kate recalled smelling the stale air of Philadelphia, and now the fresh air of Iowa. A pretty bush of bright white flowers bloomed near the depot, and she could smell its sweet perfume as well.

Mary Kate glanced at her ticket. She recalled when she first set foot on *Titanic*, how much of a novice traveler she was. In the space of a few short weeks, she had learned to fend for herself. She would make her connection here to travel north to Sioux City. She felt like she had aged in the last few weeks. She was not the same little girl her father had set loose to go to America. Nor was she as innocent now.

"Nice day, yes?" Constance smiled at Mary Kate from her window, still aboard the train. Mary Kate nodded to the older woman, who had become her friend during the last few days on their train ride together.

"I will miss you." Mary Kate smiled bravely.

"I will miss you, too. But you come to Colorado, yes?" Constance shouted as the engine hissed steam.

Mary Kate nodded again. She waved as the long black train slithered into the forest beyond her view.

Mary Kate sadly lowered her head and sighed. She walked to the depot window. "Pardon me!" she asked the tall train conductor.

"Yes, Ma'am?" he asked politely.

"Do you know when the next train leaves for Sioux City?" Mary Kate held up her ticket so he could read it.

"Probably not for another hour or two." The young man checked his pocket watch, then dumped it back in his vest pocket.

"Oh," Mary Kate sighed, "guess I'll just wait then." She walked over to a small wooden bench and plopped down. She was still wearing the same clothes she had worn on the fateful night on *Titanic*. The calico blue dress with the small pockets and long sleeves which were suddenly very unsuitable for the stuffy air. She fanned her face with her train ticket and waited patiently.

Mary Kate enjoyed the pretty scenery of Western Iowa once she was on her way again. The countryside got more lush and green all along the Missouri River. The train was not very far from Sioux City now. When she had left Philadelphia, she hadn't even thought about how she would find David when she got there. She was in such a hurry to leave that she hadn't had time to worry about the details.

Mary Kate smiled and played with the frayed hem on her dress as she thought about the delightful conversations she and Constance shared. Constance was very worldly and had lots of stories to tell. Mary Kate hoped she could make it to Colorado sometime to see her friend. Mary Kate chuckled to herself that Constance would be such a great mother.

Mary Kate's stomach twisted when she thought of never seeing her father or her brothers again. Johnny, Tommy, and Sam were probably distraught that she and Patrick had both perished on *Titanic*. What they didn't know, which was her largest source of guilt, was that she was still alive. Mary Kate's stomach tightened, she just realized the scope of what she had done. She would never again look on the face of her father or brothers! She could only think of Father Murphy's words of comfort. He had advised her that she had chosen this for herself, and she would have to live with her decision. And no one had given her as good of advice as Father Murphy, who told her she would have to make her new family from David and start with that.

Before long, the train screeched to a halt in the large station. She had no bag to carry, so she ran down the iron steps once they were lowered. She scoured all the faces waiting there and finally spied David's tall frame standing near an archway.

"David!" Mary Kate cried as she caught his attention and began to run towards him.

David ran as fast as he could across the uneven bricks to her. Mary Kate let out a high-pitched wail as David caught her in his embrace and squeezed her with all his might. She cried tears of relief and joy to have found him. He kissed her hair and hushed her.

"Don't be sad now, I've found you!" he consoled her.

Mary Kate couldn't speak, only low sobs escaped her as

onlookers stared at them inquisitively.

When Mary Kate could finally speak, she wiped her eyes with her long sleeve and smiled wearily at David. "How did you ever know that I would be here today?" she asked.

"What do you mean?" David smiled sheepishly; "I've been coming here every day since I left you in Philadelphia! I knew you would come, I just knew!" David kissed her small white hand.

"I am so lucky to have you, otherwise I could have been a slave forever!"

"Come, let's go home." David took her hand in his. Mary Kate felt warm inside when David said "home." For the first time in weeks, she finally felt that was where she was going.

Chapter 18

"Home" turned out to be a beautiful Victorian home in the heart of Sioux City. A splendid home with a widow's peak and elegant windows covered with lace curtains.

"The first thing we need to do is get you fed, then a warm bath and some new clothes," Sarah, the white-haired housemaid, told Mary Kate. Sarah was short and a little rotund, but she had the look of warmness and caring that seeped out of her every wrinkle.

"Oh, a warm bath would be wonderful right now." Mary Kate smiled at the older woman. She instantly felt "home." Just as David told her she would. Sarah brushed Mary Kate's long auburn hair and put it in a thick braid that went down the middle of her back. Night began to fall, and the air had become sultry. Mary Kate didn't feel much like eating but managed to get down a few bites. David told her he had some business, but he wanted to be with her as soon as she was rested.

After a long, hot soak in an iron clawfoot tub, Mary Kate was given her own room. It was trimmed in a dark maple wood and had two large windows with lace curtains. The view was of the Missouri River and the lush green trees sprawled along it for miles. The large four-poster bed adorned with a lace bedspread and fluffy white pillows looked so comfortable. There was a matching dresser in the same dark maple wood as well as a vanity and wardrobe. Far fancier than anything Mary Kate could have dreamed about.

"I apologize that I can only give you these three dresses for now. I plan to get you fitted for a few more appropriate outfits and hats as soon as you are up to it–" Sarah rambled on as Mary Kate looked out the large windows into the darkening Iowa sky.

"I can't thank this family enough for what they have done for me." Mary Kate finally spoke as Sarah laid a fresh white cotton nightgown on the bed.

"Well, David has spoke of nothing but you since he returned from Philadelphia. You are the only thing he's been excited about since–" Sarah realized what she was about to say and stopped.

Mary Kate smiled sympathetically at the older woman and put her hand on her plump arm. "I would be so glad if I made him happy after all he's been through." Mary Kate smiled wearily and wondered if David had told Sarah about Mary Kate's trials as well.

Sarah half-smiled and continued with her work.

Mary Kate took the nightgown and gingerly lowered it over her auburn hair. She loosened up her braid and sat at the large vanity brushing her long hair. The bath had left her so relaxed. She caressed her curls and looked at herself in the mirror. To herself, she looked much older. There seemed to be less youthfulness in her face and the beginning of forehead lines. She often wondered what her mother looked like as she entered womanhood. Did she have the same blue eyes? Was her auburn hair as thick and her hips as wide? To never have known her mother was painful enough, but perhaps being close enough to Constance over the last few days had brought up those special feelings of motherly love that Mary Kate had never really got to experience and now dreadfully longed for.

Mary Kate could see Sarah bustling about in the wardrobe, humming softly to herself. Mary Kate smiled at the older woman's actions. Sarah continued on in spite of adversity. That is what Mary Kate resolved to do. Everything happens for a reason, and she must make the most of it.

Sarah lit the lamps and excused herself from the room. Mary Kate lay wearily down in the sheets Sarah had turned down for her. She glanced at the nightstand that was occupied only by a lace doily and an oil lamp. The sheets smelled so fresh and clean, and it relaxed Mary Kate further. She wished she would stay awake for David to come home, but with no books to read or other thoughts to occupy her mind, soon her eyes drifted unwillingly into deep sleep.

The next morning, rain had invaded the landscape. It was damp yet warm as Sarah woke Mary Kate early.

"We have a lot to do today," Sarah called across the room as she opened the wardrobe doors. Mary Kate winced. What was David planning for her to do?

"Do you mean we're going to dust and clean windows?" Mary Kate asked hesitantly as the older woman pulled back her covers. Sarah chuckled in her sweet way.

"What's so funny?" Mary Kate asked defensively.

"We aren't going to do that kind of work! We're going to town to get you some new clothes!" Sarah smiled. Mary Kate had forgotten to ask Sarah about her blue calico dress. She needed the ruby ring out of the pocket, or she would surely lose it.

"Sarah, what did you do with my clothes I brought here?" Mary Kate asked in a panic.

"Oh, they are down in the wash. Why?" A confused look came over Sarah's face. Why would anyone want to keep that tattered old dress? She finished helping Mary Kate get her hair into a loose bun on top of her head.

"Could you show me where? I left something in one of the pockets."

After Mary Kate was dressed in a nice clean outfit, consisting of a starchy white blouse with a black bow tie and brown skirt, she was led to the wash room just off the kitchen in the large newer home. She grabbed the blue dress and fished through the pockets. She sighed with relief when her fingers caressed the familiar metal and ruby ring. Mary Kate quietly put it in her new skirt pocket. She didn't want Sarah to see it, because then she might have to explain its origin.

Sarah was curious but never did ask Mary Kate what she was looking for. The ladies exited the washroom and breezed through the kitchen just as David was entering the kitchen from the other side.

"Good morning!" he called out to Mary Kate and Sarah.

"Hello, David." Sarah turned toward the stove to light it.

"I am sorry I couldn't stay awake last night," Mary Kate apologized as David embraced her.

"That's all right, I was late anyway. But the good news is I may have sold six machines!" David beamed proudly. Sarah turned around and applauded, Mary Kate smiled warmly at him.

"Sarah says we are going shopping today," Mary Kate started the breakfast conversation. David nodded and set his coffee down on the saucer.

"Yes, I have asked her to take you to the dressmaker and have about a half-dozen dresses and gowns made up. Hats, too, Sarah." David smiled at the housemaid, who was more like the mother that kept the family going.

"Forgive me if I seem ungrateful, but do I really need that much?" Mary Kate asked her new family.

"I will accept nothing but the best for you, Mary Kate. You deserve it." David pushed away his breakfast plate and dabbed his mouth with his napkin.

"Well, thank you. I really don't believe I deserve all this kindness–"

"Stop, I don't want any more talking like that. You shall have everything I can give you," David interrupted, and he put his hand on Mary Kate's. She smiled at him. He was doing so well at making her feel at ease.

After breakfast, Mary Kate sat in her room for a few moments before waiting for the coach to arrive and take them to the dressmaker. She took the ruby out of her pocket and caressed it for a moment. She thought about how happy she was and felt instantly guilty. David was so nice to her and wanted to give her everything she ever wanted. Suddenly, she heard Sarah's familiar footsteps creaking on the stairs. Mary Kate hurriedly opened the drawer of her nightstand and set the ring inside. She was sitting with her hands folded in her lap when Sarah entered the room.

"Are you ready?" Sarah's face was lit up with excitement. Mary Kate nodded. Time to start making the most of it.

Chapter 19

Nearly a month had passed, and Mary Kate's days were filled with nothing but whatever she wanted to do. Sometimes it was a challenge with David gone all the time, selling the Brown family's hog-feeder machines. He undoubtedly made such a good living, but he was gone from home quite a bit.

Bored one morning, Mary Kate started to pick things up from David's desk. One letter in particular caught her interest. Her mouth fell open as she read the words. It was from a young woman named Suzanne. The letter said how wonderful it was that David was home and how anxious she would be when they could court again.

A sick feeling overtook her. She had never thought to inquire of Sarah or David as to whether or not David may have a love interest. How rude of her to interrupt! Mary Kate ran towards the kitchen, tears stinging her eyes all the way there.

"Sarah!" Mary Kate cried, bursting into the kitchen. Sarah looked up from the stove with shock and horror to see her young friend in such dismay.

"Mary Kate!" Sarah wrapped her hands, still coated in flour, around the hysterical woman.

"Sarah! Please tell me! Have I been stupid?"

"What in the world is going on?"

"Who is Suzanne?"

Sarah released Mary Kate and rolled her eyes. She leaned up against the sink.

"Suzanne is the neighbor girl. She's been in love with David

155

since she turned boy-crazy at the age of thirteen. I wouldn't worry about her," Sarah explained nonchalantly.

"Have she and David ever courted?" Mary Kate wiped her subsiding tears.

"Well ... yes. Once before he went to England, but pay it no mind," Sarah tried to reassure Mary Kate in vain.

"Oh, Sarah! I've just been so stupid!" Mary Kate cried, and she ran up the stairs. She began to collect things in a large bag that lay open on the bed. Tears spilled down her flushed cheeks as she pulled open the drawers and emptied them one garment at a time into the bag. The sobs were unrelenting as she cursed herself silently.

I'm so stupid! David must think I'm an idiot! I can't believe this is happening! Oh, why did I come here? She plagued herself over and over again as the jealousy imprisoned her heart.

David had returned home a few moments before and couldn't find Sarah or Mary Kate downstairs. He stood confused and silent in the doorway to Mary Kate's room, watching as she hurled things into a large bag.

"Are you going somewhere?" he asked her, his arms folded across his chest, watching her with curiosity, oblivious to anything that had happened. David feared Mary Kate was preparing herself to return to Ireland, and he rushed to her and put his hand over hers.

"Don't go!" his blue eyes pleaded.

"Why couldn't I see it?" Mary Kate's eyes flooded over.

"See what?" David was flabbergasted at the show of emotion.

"Suzanne." That one word tasted like poison on Mary Kate's lips.

David blinked and looked at her as if she were a stranger. Mary Kate found it difficult to read his reaction. He didn't act shocked as if he tried to deny his feelings, but he didn't speak for several moments.

"If I knew you were in love with her, I wouldn't have come here at all." Mary Kate flung herself on the bed and buried her sobbing face into the pillow.

David sat on the edge of the bed and stared at his feet while she cried.

"I'm sorry, I should never have come here. I was so confused and I must have … imagined something!" Mary Kate was hysterical and was making no sense.

David still stared at only his feet. The little bit of courting that had happened with Suzanne was something he had forgotten about once he had met Virginia. He sighed and stood up. "How did you learn of her?"

"I found the letter."

His stomach sank. "Oh." David said plainly.

"I will leave. I won't interfere."

"Mary Kate!" David chastised her.

"Well, please then, just tell me. I was foolish to come here! I'm sorry, maybe I was thinking there was something. I should never have come." Mary Kate shook her head, her face still down in her pillow.

"Oh." David left the room. His distant reaction made her eyes cry even harder. So then it was true! For all the things she had been through recently, this was by far the worst. Matthew had loved her and no one else! How could Mary Kate believe that David would love her too? She was so foolish and childish to assume that he would love her and take care of her. The thought of living in a house where she was a permanent house guest with David and his wife was worse than being made a house-servant by the Burnes!

Mary Kate cried herself to sleep; something she hadn't done in months. David was probably rushing to Suzanne now, and the mere thought of it made Mary Kate tremble with bitterness.

David peeked in on Mary Kate early in the morning. He had to leave today for Missouri. Gone a week at least, maybe two. He bit his lip in guilt. Why should he feel guilty? He had done nothing wrong. He had known Suzanne long before Mary Kate. Suzanne had also promised to stay away since David had written her about Virginia. Suzanne must've heard that Virginia had died, and now she also was confused about the young woman staying at his home.

David knew he had a decision that lay before him. He loved Mary Kate dearly. She was special and kind and everything a woman should be. Suzanne was of his class, though. Raised very rich and very used to getting what she wanted. How would she take it that she couldn't buy David's love?

David wanted to wake Mary Kate. He had to go, for the train left at seven. David knew that there was not enough time to disturb her from her sleep and explain. Hating him would be the worst thing that Mary Kate could do to hurt him. Woefully, he picked up his leather bag and left.

"Take care of her, Sarah." He kissed the maid's wrinkled face before putting on his hat and coat in the foyer.

"I will," Sarah reassured him with a pat on the back.

"I will be back soon."

"I know, but you'd better do something before this all falls apart in your hands."

"Yes, I know." David shut the door behind him. He sighed and headed down the walk to the waiting carriage.

The evening rainstorm was welcome relief from the past few weeks' oppressive summer heat.

Mary Kate sat on the bed, her legs drawn up to her chest. She rested her head on her knees as lightning split open the Iowa sky.

David was gone on another one of his trips. South to Missouri to sell more of the hog feeders that Matthew's grandfather had patented. Often she wondered what she was doing here with David gone so much. Sarah was good company, but Mary Kate knew nothing of Iowa or Sioux City. David was very apprehensive to just let her walk about town by herself, but if he were never there, what was she to do? Being so lonely and bored all the time always let her mind drift back to the same thing. Could she live the rest of her life this way? Wondering and waiting for David to come back from each trip, just as she had fully expected Matthew to return from the icy depths? The fact that he had left under such awful circumstances had not made it any easier this time. Mary Kate was still very upset about the whole Suzanne incident and David's reluctance to talk about it.

Mary Kate squeezed her eyes shut. She had to make David understand that something had to change. He could take his trips and sell his machines, but Mary Kate had to *do* something in his absence. She could no longer sit idle and watch the rain pour down into the street.

Mary Kate lay flat on the bed as the thunder hammered outside. She tried to close her eyes and force herself to sleep, but it never settled in.

Sarah's familiar voice called from down the hall. Mary Kate leapt from the bed and ran to the door.

"Sarah! What is it?"

"David's home!" Sarah cried excitedly.

"Oh!" Mary Kate's heart leapt as she came down the steps. As she put her foot on the bottom step, David came into the foyer. His hat and coat were soaked, and rain dripped from the brim of his cap. He was handsome, and it could be very easy to forget why she was so upset.

Mary Kate felt guilty about her earlier thoughts. She was being selfish. David traveled and worked so much, and for her to demand that he give her something to keep herself busy seemed rather childish now. She smiled at him warmly.

"Well, look there! She stuck around!" David mocked her as he removed his hat and coat. Mary Kate felt almost invaded as though he could read her innermost thoughts.

"I almost ran away," she joked back, though her stomach bubbled over with nerves. Sarah brushed the water off of his garments and then hurried off to the kitchen. David never took his eyes off of Mary Kate. What would he say? He couldn't ignore the terrible night that happened just before he left.

"I have supper waiting on the stove," Sarah announced, waddling back into the foyer. She gave a curious look to the two young people. Mary Kate stood by the banister staring at David as he returned the young woman's stare from the door.

"After you." David motioned for Mary Kate to go ahead. She smiled shyly and followed Sarah to the kitchen.

Most of their meals were shared at the small kitchen table instead of the large dining room. Tonight, however, Mary Kate didn't feel comfortable in such close quarters.

"Sit next to me, Mary Kate." David pulled out a chair and motioned for her to sit.

"All right." Mary Kate sat and scooted towards the table. Her eyes shifted toward the stove as she watched Sarah fill the plates, anything to avoid eye contact with David. Sarah brought the steaming plates over and then wiped her hands on her apron.

"Good night, my kittens." Sarah kissed Mary Kate's cheek, and the young girl's eyes widened.

"You aren't really going to bed, are you?" Mary Kate stood up from her chair.

David also rose from his seat. "I've asked her to leave us alone together."

"Oh." Mary Kate looked down at the table and swallowed the lump in her throat. She knew something was about to happen. Perhaps David felt it was time for her to move on. The uncertainty made Mary Kate feel out of control, similar to the way she felt … that night! It always invaded her thoughts!

"Good night," Sarah repeated, and she disappeared through the kitchen door. Mary Kate resumed her seat nervously.

"Did you travel well?" Mary Kate made idle chatter, trying to distract her thoughts.

"Yes, definitely." David smiled at her.

"Very good." Mary Kate set down her fork, eating was not her first priority right now.

"Mary Kate…." David sighed seriously as he pushed his plate away.

Mary Kate looked down at her hands, her heart raced. "Yes?"

David reached over and took her hand. Mary Kate looked at the two of their hands clasped together. He rubbed the back of her hand gently with his thumb. "I was wondering…."

"David, you are sweating."

"I know, what I'm trying to say…."

Mary Kate's eyes searched David's nervous demeanor. She was starting to draw her own conclusions.

"Mary Kate, what would you think if you could live here forever?"

"Oh, I would like that."

"Would you?"

"Well, yes…." Mary Kate stood up and held on to the back of the chair as she spoke, "But David, when you go away, I can't stand it. I'm so bored. And I won't live here if Suzanne is the one you intend to be with. I don't know anyone but you or Sarah. If I'm going to stay, I'm going to need something to do."

David stared at her blankly. "Hmm." He scratched his chin.

"I'm sorry, David. I do love living here." Mary Kate sat down again and grabbed his hand.

"No, you're right. I've been so foolish just to leave you here and expect you to keep yourself busy. We'll find something." David patted her hand.

"Thank you. I don't mean to be childish or ungrateful."

"You're not! Don't be silly. I can assure you that."

"I just miss you when you are away."

"I miss you also, Mary Kate."

"You do?"

"Yes, I missed you this time especially, and I had something to ask you before I left, but I decided to wait until I returned."

Mary Kate raised her eyebrows curiously.

"Marry me, Mary Kate."

Her eyes widened with surprise. "David! I didn't realize! I mean...." She was speechless.

"So is that 'yes'?"

"Yes!" Mary Kate cried out. They both jumped up and hugged each other. A mixed confusion of emotions filled her. This was not the life Mary Kate thought she would have, but strangely, it felt right.

Sarah smiled from her perch on the stairs and quickly glided back up to her room.

Chapter 20

Mary Kate stood nervously by the door. In a few minutes, she would be walking down the garden pathway to the fountain to hold David's hand in matrimony. Sarah fussed busily with Mary Kate's dress and veil, while Mary Kate couldn't help but think of the last few months. The whole reason she was on that ship was to be married to William Richter, would her wedding day to him have been this happy? Would she have stood so nervously by the door peaking at her soon-to-be husband?

Instantly, Matthew came to mind, and Mary Kate cursed herself for thinking of him on her and David's wedding day. She knew she must try to forget or not even think about if Matthew had lived. There was no use in fantasizing about something that would never come true. But a curious part of her couldn't help but wonder what her and Matthew's wedding would have been like. Mary Kate knew without hesitation that she would have been so anxious to be married to him. She closed her eyes and sighed as Sarah gave her long train one final tug. Mary Kate smiled at her older friend and looked down at the ground guiltily. If only her father and brothers could see her.

"I need more hairpins. I'll be right back, dear." Sarah was out the door before it could creak to a halt just before it latched. Mary Kate knelt down in front of the only chair in the room. She lowered her head into her hands and prayed. She prayed for God to forgive her for the guilt that still consumed her when she thought about her family back in Ireland. She prayed for her brother Patrick to forgive her and watch over her and the rest of their family at home. She silently pleaded Patrick to also take care of her as he always had, even up to his last moment.

Sarah returned to find Mary Kate slumped over the seat of the chair. She gasped and ran to her.

"Mary Katherine!" Sarah cried as she pulled back the young girl from the chair to find her blue eyes red with tears.

Sarah hugged Mary Kate relentlessly for a few minutes before speaking. "Aren't you happy to marry David?"

"Of course I am, Sarah. It's just … everything else that's happened. I have just become overwhelmed by everything since April. When I was alone, I was thinking about my family and.…" Mary Kate squeezed her eyes shut.

"Listen, dear," Sarah held Mary Kate's hands with her own, "you are making your own family starting today. Please be happy," Sarah begged.

"Don't you worry, I have every intention of marrying David and being completely happy." Mary Kate chuckled and sniffled at the same time.

"Well, I was going to give this to you right before you walked down the aisle, but you look like you could use it now." Sarah pulled a delicate lace and cotton handkerchief out of her bag. Mary Kate reveled in its delicate beauty and hugged her friend.

"I made it for you, and I've put your new initials on it." Sarah beamed proudly, and Mary Kate smiled happily as she noticed the embroidered letters, MKW.

"Thank you." Mary Kate peeked out the door again. She could see David, though he couldn't see her. He nervously stood in his best suit and checked his pocket watch again. Mary Kate had to suppress a giggle at his nervousness.

A knock came from the other side of the cottage. Father Murphy entered and smiled at Mary Kate.

"Now, don't you look pretty," he told her as he sauntered

across the small cottage to her. Mary Kate beamed happily as the priest helped her put her veil over her heart-shaped face. He pulled out his small bible from under his robe and chanted a small prayer over her. He had come all the way from Philadelphia at David's special request.

"Amen." Mary Kate and Father Murphy both made the sign of the cross at his completion of the prayer. Father Murphy's chubby red cheeks glowed as he smiled at the bride-to-be.

"Are you nervous, Mary Kate?" he asked the young woman he had become so fond of when she was in Philadelphia. Mary Kate shrugged her shoulders and simply smiled. Father Murphy put a reassuring arm around her and laughed merrily.

"It happens to a lot of brides, I assure you. Not to worry." Father Murphy winked over at Sarah. The bell in the garden chimed one o'clock. It was time.

The wedding ceremony went smoothly, and Mary Kate felt transformed as the ceremony was near its end. She and David locked hands and gazed into each other's eyes lovingly.

"You may kiss the bride!" Father Murphy smiled at them and pushed them together with his strong arms. Mary Kate couldn't help but grin. She never thought about actually kissing David. But he was her husband now.

David lowered his head to her warm face and kissed her softly and quickly. Before she knew it, it was over with and they were disembarking on their journey down the aisle as husband and wife.

A small party ensued with ham, dressing, and cake. Mary Kate met a flurry of people she had never seen before. She recognized Virginia and Matthew's grandfather, Mr. Brown. He approached her when she was standing by herself in the garden for a few minutes of solitude. Mary Kate stood erect, nervously waiting what Mr. Brown would say. Could he be as cruel and arrogant as his daughter's family, the Burnes?

"Young lady." Mr. Brown smiled mischievously, his face turning red from his pointy chin all the way to the top of his balding head. He stood right in front of Mary Kate now, his hands clasped behind his back. Mary Kate's breath quickened.

"Yes, Sir?" she said in a whisper.

"Congratulations to you."

"Thank you." Mary Kate smiled appreciatively. He shifted his stance and looked at the grass.

"I heard about you, you know."

Mary Kate's heart was pounding furiously in her chest. "Oh?"

"Yes, my daughter–"

"She enslaved me cruelly, and I cannot forgive her or her husband, I'm sorry!" Mary Kate exploded defensively. She turned to run away from Mr. Brown, but he gently took her arm.

"Don't run away, I know what they did to you. I mean to tell you I don't agree with it. David told me how they treated you, and he also told me about how you and Matthew loved each other. I want to say how pitifully sorry I am about everything you've been subjected to in the last six months." Mr. Brown turned his blue eyes toward the young woman.

"You are?"

"Yes, I am. I loved my granddaughter, Mrs. Worthington. I was so worried about David when that damn ship went down. I wasn't sure if he would ever find anyone he felt about like he did with Virginia. I'm sorry if that seems painful for me to say, but…."

"No, not at all, Mr. Brown. I met Virginia, and I liked her very much. She was a good person, and very honest and forthright. I can see why David would have loved her so."

"Well, yes, she was very strong-willed." Mr. Brown chuckled, his round belly shaking.

Mary Kate smiled and lowered her eyes. Mr. Brown was the

first person to call her Mrs. Worthington.

"I also know that Matthew was a very loving person, and I think you and he would have made a great match if only...." The look in Mr. Brown's eyes was far away now.

David came down the path, his eyes twinkling when he saw his new wife.

"Congratulations, David!" Mr. Brown called as David approached them, thankful to be happy in the moment. Mr. Brown clapped his best salesman on the back.

"Thank you, Sir." David shook the older man's hand.

"The best to you both always." Mr. Brown kissed Mary Kate's hand and left them alone in the garden. David beamed down at his bride and took her hand.

"Is everyone still here?" Mary Kate questioned.

"Yes, but it's getting dark. Soon everyone will go home." David winked at Mary Kate, and she grinned. She knew what he was thinking. Mary Kate knew that the kiss today at their wedding would probably turn into more later. Sarah had given her a talk about what usually happens on a man and woman's wedding night, although Mary Kate had already known somewhat from listening to her family talk and reading books. She wondered what David was thinking of tonight and what might happen.

Several more hours passed, and the party broke up. The car took Mary Kate and David back to the home that was now theirs as husband and wife. Sarah had promised she would stay at her friends' tonight, so that the young couple could be alone.

"It's very quiet in here." Mary Kate laughed. All of a sudden, she felt very shy.

"Yes," was all David said as he opened the window.

"Is it always still this warm in October?" Mary Kate made idle conversation, trying to keep her mind off of the anticipation.

"Sometimes," David said again as he walked towards her.

He scooped her up into his arms, and she gasped, then they both burst out laughing as he carried her up the stairs.

Mary Kate slipped into her own room to change out of her dress. She managed to get the corset off and the veil that was woven into her long auburn hair. She had just slipped the shimmering nightgown over her head when David opened the door. He stood there in only his pants with his bare feet. He was so tall, and to see him in such a state brought a smile to Mary Kate's face.

"What, do I look funny?" David laughed.

"Yes, you do!" Mary Kate giggled as he made his way over to her and sat down with her on the bed. Her heart was pounding so hard she thought it would come through her body.

"Hold me, David," Mary Kate whispered as David wrapped his strong arms around her and pulled her close. He nuzzled into her warm hair, and Mary Kate closed her eyes. She wasn't sure what was going to happen, but her stomach felt fluttery, and she tried to put the thought out of her mind of the first time that she kissed Matthew. She knew she shouldn't compare anything that would happen with David to what she always wondered would happen with Matthew.

David lowered his head but stopped just short of kissing her.

"I'm sorry," Mary Kate sighed.

"Why are you apologizing?" David smiled.

"This is incredibly hard for us both, I think."

David nodded in agreement. "We don't have to do anything. We could just lie here all night like this."

"Is that what you want?" Mary Kate whispered.

"Well, not exactly." David chuckled. He had such anticipation about tonight after kissing her for the first time at their wedding. The soft white flowers that dotted her hair and the long white gown she wore. The way her rosy cheeks glowed in the afternoon's hot sunshine. He wasn't sure if she was ready, but he had been ready for her for quite some time.

Drawing David near to her, Mary Kate smiled. This time he bent his head to kiss her, and he did not stop. He softly kissed her rose pink lips. His warm breath brought out feelings in her that she thought she had lost when she lost Matthew. She wanted David to kiss her now, and she kissed him back. She ran her fingers through his jet-black hair. His desire rose as she responded to his touch, and he hungrily pulled her to him. She did not feel guilt, but a strange sense of freedom like a bird being set loose from its cage. She let David guide her, he had brought her into his life, and now he was putting the past behind them and helping them both move onward.

Chapter 21

Married life was easy, and Mary Kate relieved her boredom when David was away by resuming her passion of reading. He had purchased several new volumes for her that kept her occupied when she wasn't helping Sarah.

The evening air was beginning to turn crisp, and Mary Kate reveled in the splendid colors of fall that graced her eyes. The change of seasons here was amazing to her. Each one had its own elegance. Snuggling down into the covers, Mary Kate reached over and pulled the nightstand drawer open to put her book away. A familiar gold glint caught her eyes. The ruby! Her heart thumping, she pulled it out of the drawer and gingerly looked at it.

Abruptly, David walked into the room, home early from his latest trip. Mary Kate's eyes bulged, and she quickly put her hands behind her back.

"Mary Kate? What are you hiding?" David smiled, thinking it was a game.

"Nothing!" Mary Kate's eyes shifted to the floor. David stared at her curiously.

"You can tell me."

"Nothing, I say." Mary Kate smiled timidly.

"Show me then, if it's nothing."

"I can't show you."

"Show me!" David was becoming anxious.

Mary Kate gasped as he came up to her and pulled her arms out from behind her back.

"Open your hand. I beg you, I can't bear to know you are hiding something from me!" David cried, suddenly angry.

Mary Kate didn't want to show him the ring. It would hurt him too badly. He would think she was still in love with Matthew even though they had been married to each other for well over a month now and *Titanic* had sunk nearly eight months ago.

David grabbed her hand and forced her thin fingers open. His mouth gaped open when he realized what she was holding in her palm. He plucked it out of her hand, and Mary Kate stared at him, wide-eyed.

"David, listen!" Mary Kate took her husband's arm.

"Why were you hiding this from me?" David questioned her despondently.

"I just thought that, well, that it would hurt your feelings if you knew I kept it."

"So you lied to me?"

"I didn't lie, I just didn't tell you about it. I forgot I had it."

"I don't know. I don't know what to do about it." David shook his head.

"I am so sorry. You know I love you. I wouldn't have married you if I didn't," Mary Kate cried, trying to get David to meet her eyes.

"Mary Kate, please tell me you want to forget what happened last April."

"I do want to forget, but David, I can't!" Mary Kate wailed.

"I know we can't forget but, please," David put the ring in his pocket and held his new wife closely," I just want us to stop living as if we are still aboard that ship! I just want us to be happy together, here in this place! Not in some distant dream that will never come true."

"What should we do? Do with the ring? Do with our lives?"

"I just want to be with you, I know we can never forget, but we can go on."

"Do you promise?"

"Of course." David sighed and walked over to the window. Mary Kate gulped. What if he threw the ring out? He only stared out the window blankly.

"It's getting cold in here. I will have Sarah light the fireplace. Good night." David did not even meet her eyes before leaving the room.

Mary Kate knew she had hurt him, and she sighed. David probably thought that she thought about Matthew every time they kissed or made love. She didn't know how to show him that it wasn't true. She would leave him alone until the morning, maybe then she could explain about the ring.

When Sarah entered the room, she startled Mary Kate, who jumped.

"Sorry, Ma'am, I didn't mean to scare you." Sarah apologized.

"You didn't scare me, Sarah. Sometimes I only scare myself." Mary Kate sat on the bed, and Sarah chuckled as she struck the match to the kindling.

"I think I really made David mad tonight," Mary Kate confessed.

"Oh," was Sarah's only response as she fanned the flames to feed the fire.

"What do you think I should do?" Mary Kate sat on the bed and threw her long braid behind her back.

"I think you should just give him a little time," Sarah advised, then walked over to Mary Kate. She put her arms around the young woman, who stood a foot taller than she did. The women embraced, like they were mother and daughter.

Mary Kate smiled down at her friend and thanked her for her advice. Sarah had become like her mother in the last few months. They had shared secrets and stories over tea. Mary Kate still missed Constance dreadfully, but Sarah was the best stand-in a girl could find for a mother.

Mary Kate woke to the sound of someone stoking the fire. She looked up and, through the amber glow of the fire, saw her husband.

"David!" Mary Kate sat up in bed. He came and sat on the edge of the four-poster bed.

"I thought you were still mad at me," Mary Kate said hesitantly.

"I couldn't stay mad at you." David wrapped his arms around his wife.

"I just didn't want you to think that I don't love you." Mary Kate kissed his cheek.

"I know you do. I shouldn't have been so tyrannical." David moved his hands over Mary Kate's shapely waist. Mary Kate buried her head into his strong shoulder and sighed with relief. David began to kiss her face softly and stroked her soft hair. They could feel what was going to happen next, it was strong enough to wash away both their fears of anything that happened last April and make them temporarily forget about the ruby.

As the days passed, Mary Kate became used to her new life with David. It was Christmas morning, and Mary Kate giggled mischievously when she thought of the perfect gift she and Sarah had thought of for David. He would definitely be surprised.

After church that morning, no one was hungry. Mary Kate couldn't wait to give David his surprise. They sat by the large evergreen tree in the parlor. It was decked with candles and beautiful glass ornaments that David and Mary Kate had purchased together.

"Let me go first!" David begged as he handed Mary Kate a small package. It was heavy and prettily wrapped with a nice bow. Her long fingers untied the bow and opened the box. Inside was a rock. Mary Kate laughed. Sarah chuckled mischievously.

"How thoughtful of you, my dear," Mary Kate said sarcastically.

"Do you know what it means?"

"No, please tell me," Mary Kate smiled and retorted again with sarcasm.

"There are mountains. Rocky Mountains."

"Oh...." Mary Kate was intrigued and a little bewildered. She couldn't quite understand what David was trying to tell her.

"That's what they call the mountains in Colorado." David said blankly, waiting for Mary Kate's reaction. She smiled and caressed her rock.

She gave David a dry smile. "You mean, we get to go see Constance?"

"Yes, probably not until the railway opens through the mountains in spring, maybe May or June."

"You are so wonderful!" Mary Kate exclaimed and jumped up to kiss her husband. Sarah smiled and clapped her hands.

Mary Kate and Sarah exchanged impish glances, and Mary Kate handed David a large box with a nice tie that Sarah had made for her.

David lifted the lid to the box. He gasped and then looked over to his wife. "Truly?" he said, breathless.

Mary Kate and Sarah both nodded. David jumped off his seat and ran over to his wife. He held her and kissed her tenderly as they began to weep with happiness. Sarah held both their hands and laughed happily with them.

The smallest pair of baby booties either of them had seen was then carefully placed in the room that was to become the nursery.

Chapter 22

It was dark as the coach pulled up in front of a large brownstone home just as Constance came running outside. She was waving her arms frantically in the air.

"Mary Kate! David! You're here!" she cried as she pulled open the door to the coach before the driver even had a chance to dismount.

David exited first, then held out his hand. He smirked at Constance, she was not aware they were expecting. Mary Kate wobbled down the carriage steps as Contance's jaw dropped. Then the two women began to laugh and cry at the same time as they fell in each other's arms.

"I'm so happy for you!" Constance wiped her eyes with her dress sleeve. She helped Mary Kate up the stairs as David helped the driver with the bags.

Contance's home was large and filled to the brim with books and little pieces of projects that appeared to always have good starts but never quite made it to completion. The kitchen, in which they now stood, was large, and cupboards went from the floor to the ceiling on every wall, stuffed top to bottom with everything imaginable.

"Would you like some tea or coffee after your long journey?" Constance set a kettle to boil on the stove.

"That would be wonderful." Mary Kate sighed with exhaustion.

"You look like you could use a good night's sleep. Well not to worry, a couple nights of this fresh mountain air and you'll be refreshed in no time." Constance smiled at her young friend.

"The train ride was so long. And bumpy!" Mary Kate laughed as she held the round protrusion of her waist. Constance reached out and patted her young friend's hand. David yawned and stretched in the straightback kitchen chair.

"David, why don't I have Henry show you to your room?" Constance stood up and rang the kitchen bell, and within seconds a young Asian boy entered. David yawned again and only nodded in agreement.

"Would you please show Mr. Worthington to his room?" David kissed Mary Kate good night and gave Constance a long squeeze before disappearing out of the kitchen.

"So...." Constance smiled playfully. The kettle whistled and she stood up to pour the tea.

"Oh, so many things have happened since I saw you last." Mary Kate removed her shoes from her swollen feet.

"I can see that!" Constance remarked about Mary Kate's expanding waistline.

"Yes, that being the most important."

"I'm so sorry I couldn't make it back for your wedding, but you can see how long a train ride it is," Constance apologized as she brought two steaming teacups to the table.

"Constance, we understand, but we do wish you could have been there." Mary Kate yawned also and leaned back in the chair.

The baby leapt with her first drink of tea, and Mary Kate laughed at the tickling inside her body.

Constance tucked her dark red hair behind her ears and laughed, her hands wrapped around her teacup. "Did you see the mountains yet?" Constance sipped the hot tea. Her familiar wrinkles were a welcome sight.

"No, it was too dark."

"Well, you can see them in the morning, they are majestic indeed."

"I can't wait. I want so much to be here with you."

"I'm so glad you came. Maybe the nightmares can stop now that I know someone that understands them." Constance looked down at the wooden table with woe.

"Constance, there isn't a day that goes by that I don't think about April."

"I know. Me also."

"Would you think I'm a bad person if I tell you something?" Mary Kate leaned forward and whispered.

"No, I've told you before you can tell me anything."

"Not a day goes by that I don't think about *Titanic*, or Matthew, or my brother. Is there something wrong with me?" Mary Kate asked her friend poignantly.

"No, there is nothing wrong with that, love. It would be unnatural if you didn't. You are human, and none of us there that night will ever forget. Not until the day we die and even then...." Constance leaned back in her chair, closed her eyes, and shook her head.

"No, we won't ever forget. It would be a dishonor to those we loved, but let's be happy we have found each other." Constance reached across the table and took Mary Kate's hand.

Mary Kate smiled tenderly at the woman she cared so much about and yawned.

"You must be tired, I'm taking you to bed!" Constance laughed and spoke to Mary Kate like she was her own child, which filled Mary Kate's heart with glee.

Mary Kate entered the dark room and fumbled towards the bed. She could hear David snoring softly, and she sat down as she felt the soft covers that adorned the mattress.

David turned towards her and snorted in his sleep as he heard her climb in the soft sheets. Mary Kate snuggled against him and yawned again.

"Mary Kate?" David asked suddenly.

"Yes?" she answered sleepily.

"I found that ring in my overnight case. I forgot I had put it there." Mary Kate's heart leapt. She always wondered where he had put it or if he had disposed of it.

"Maybe we should have given it to Mr. Brown or, oh, I don't know," David muttered, and he fell back asleep. Mary Kate turned the other way from David and let tears silently stream down her cheeks as she came to a decision. She knew that if she and David were ever to completely heal, the ruby must cease to be a part of their lives.

The long climb up the mountain was strenuous. The air was definitely thinner, which made it hard for Mary Kate to catch her breath. Sometimes the loose rocks would slip from underneath Mary Kate's feet, but David was always there to catch her. Just has he always had every other time she faltered, no matter what the circumstances. Mary Kate smiled at him. She really did love him. She wasn't sure at first if she could and at first wondered if they were just clinging to each other because of everything that they had been through together.

When she lay awake at night sometimes, the last year of her life didn't seem real. Matthew didn't seem real. Her life in Ireland didn't seem real. In the last few weeks, Mary Kate suddenly felt real and alive again. She thought of her baby growing inside her and the new love she had grown for David. Things were finally developing into the new life she had chosen.

Mary Kate tossed the ring with an unwilling heart. For an instant, as it left her hand, she wished she could grasp it back. To her, the ring *was* Matthew. She could still see his clean-shaven face that kissed her for the first time, and it still haunted her dreams. The five-o-clock shadow face that said good-bye to her from *Titanic*. She could still hear his voice "I will not rest until I find you … and I will not forget. I promise." Only his memories had survived, and sometimes in her sleep, she could hear his voice and feel his kiss. Mary Kate also thought about Patrick, she didn't want to think about him being trapped in the ship with no chance. She closed her eyes, and she could still feel her brother's rough red beard scratching her face as he gave her his last kiss. The baby leapt in her stomach, as if sensing its mother's emotion.

David stood behind her and did not smile. He knew what the ruby meant to her. The ring symbolized Matthew and everything that he meant to her in the short time that she knew him. Tears sprang to David's eyes. The ruby was, to all three of them, the symbol of what had changed their lives forever.

David too had lost something very precious to himself. After the wreck, he had thought very little about Virginia. He closed it out of his mind as if to keep the pain from coming. A very little part of it still didn't seem real to him. The ocean had swallowed the largest ship in the whole world. The ocean had taken all of his possessions and all of his heart when it took Virginia as it went down. David was sure he would never be happy again, and he squeezed his eyes shut, trying to put the pain out of his memory. He was glad in a way about what happened. It brought him Mary Kate, and of course their baby would never have happened if things turned out as originally planned. Fate had worked its course.

Mary Kate turned around with glossy blue eyes. She still couldn't believe that Matthew was gone. It was fate they had met, and fate that saw to it they were parted. His face was only a sad memory to her now. He went out of her life almost as quickly as he had come into it, and she felt a little strange that maybe she had imagined him and everything else about *Titanic*. She looked down the mountainside. The tall fir trees jutted up in the sky all the way down. They could hear the rushing of the nearby stream over the perfectly placed rocks. Constance was right. Colorado was the most beautiful place Mary Kate had ever been to. She only wished fate had brought her here some other way.

Constance smiled to herself. Mary Kate and David were nice together. If it weren't for *Titanic*, they wouldn't have had anything much in common. Now they seemed so at ease with each other. So warm and loving. Not passionate, but sincere. Things for Constance would never be the same again with Reggie gone. Her hazel eyes welled up when she thought about the last time she saw him, standing by the rail, helping other women into lifeboats. That was his way though, helping others until the end.

David let Mary Kate fall graciously into his warm embrace. He closed his eyes and rested his chin on top of her auburn head. He beckoned Constance silently to come over, too. The three embraced and cried for a little while as the ruby made its final journey.

EPILOGUE

No breeze could penetrate the warm August Iowa night. Mary Kate sweated and sighed impatiently as the pains came and went. David squeezed her hand tightly, and he smiled excitedly at her. Soon their baby would come into the world.

"Do you need anything?" Sarah looked worried as she wiped the sweat from Mary Kate's clammy white forehead. Mary Kate shook her head as another pain came, and she gritted her teeth through it. David smiled warmly at her and patted her soft hair that was soaked in sweat. The locusts played their tune through the open window that sultry night. He sat back in the wooden chair next to the bed. "We never did decide on a name," he said hesitantly.

"Didn't we pick Matthew for a boy or Virginia for a girl?" Mary Kate panted.

"Yes. I was wondering though, isn't that holding on to the past a bit much?" David asked thoughtfully, as another labor pain came down on Mary Kate.

"I suppose you are right." Mary Kate was out of breath again.

"Well, I don't mean to hurt your feelings if you had your heart set on it...." David squeezed her hand as Mary Kate shook her head.

"You are right, David. We are holding on to the past. We need to move on with our life together."

"What name would be appropriate than?" David rubbed her hand softly.

The name never did get decided on until the next morning. The sun began to bear down on the Iowa prairie again as an infant's cry pierced the heavy air that began to lay morning dew on the grass.

"A boy!" David cried happily. Mary Kate wept tears of joy. Finally someone of her own flesh and blood she could hold close to her again. Sarah stood by proudly.

The infant slept soundly in his mother's arms. Mary Kate touched his small nose and remarked how much like his father he looked.

"I think his hair is a bit red though," David teased his wife.

"Do you like Constance?" Mary Kate asked, looking up into her husband's tanned face inquisitively.

"Of course I like Constance don't be silly."

"No, I mean the *name* Constance." When David realized what she meant, a smile spread over his face like wildfire.

"Constance for a boy?" David asked, still smiling.

"Yes, Constance is common for a boy or girl in Ireland," Mary Kate explained.

"Yes, Constance. Constance Patrick Worthington. I like that very much. What should we call him for short?" David laughed.

"We can decide that later, for now let's call him "ours." David bent down to kiss his wife softly on her lips. The circle that had brought them here together had been rough. But it was now complete.

*